THE ODDS

JEFF STRAND

For more information about the author, visit http://www.JeffStrand.com

Subscribe to Jeff Strand's free monthly newsletter (which includes a brand-new original short story in every issue) at
http://eepurl.com/bpv5br

ISBN: 9798640737851

1

Don't do it, Ethan Caustin thought. *Don't you dare do it. You'll hate yourself.*

He shouldn't have even brought his credit cards into the casino. Hell, he shouldn't have gone in here in the first place. He should have been the kind of person who learned from his horrible mistakes. The kind of person who *didn't* lose several thousand dollars that he couldn't come anywhere close to being able to afford. The kind of person who knew that "I'll spend fifty bucks, maximum, and if I lose it all, I'm done" was a lie.

This whole business trip was a mistake. The hotel where he was staying didn't have a casino, but it was a quick walk to the nearest one. The trip wasn't mandatory. They could've found somebody else to go in his place. Somebody who wouldn't destroy their life.

Don't get a cash advance. Don't take the card out of your wallet. Go back to your hotel.

There was a 1-800 number displayed that he could call for

gambling addiction. He wondered if they could talk him out of sticking his credit card into the machine the same way somebody on the other end might talk somebody out of leaping off a tall building.

Leaping off a building didn't sound so bad right now.

Jenny was going to kill him.

Or just be heartbroken. Give him a look of pity, or a look of disgust. She'd wonder how she had the misfortune of marrying a loser with absolutely no self-control. Gambling wasn't even fun. It's not like he was enjoying himself as he played the high roller slot machines. Sure, there was an adrenaline rush when he won, but the experience wasn't *fun.* He could've spent way less and took a ride on the zipline.

He needed to take another look at the note again.

Normally he kept it tucked into his wallet, but he'd put it in his pocket after reading it several times since walking into the casino. A faded note on hotel stationary, written to himself eight years ago.

Dear Ethan,

This is to remind you of how utterly shitty you feel right now. The self-loathing might fade, but right now you'd give anything to be able to take it all back. Remember this feeling the next time you want to throw away money in a slot machine. YOU ARE MISERABLE.

The note had worked in the past. Not today.

He looked at it again.

It was, of course, too late. The damage was done.

Don't get a cash advance.

The conundrum here was that putting his credit card into the machine offered a chance for redemption. He could win it all back. And honestly, with as much as he'd lost, did a little more even matter?

"Honey, I lost seven thousand dollars," would not get him in less trouble than "Honey, I lost nine thousand dollars." Ten thousand was worse, sure. That was a whole new level. But if he kept it under ten, there was no real difference between seven thousand and nine thousand. If he stopped now, he'd have to tearfully confess to Jenny that he lost the seven grand. If he kept going, he might not have to confess anything.

It was ridiculous to stop now, when he could still fix this.

His luck was bound to turn around. How long could his losing streak possibly last?

He'd have to be an idiot *not* to get the cash advance.

No.

He was trying to justify further appalling behavior. He needed to quit now. He needed to walk right the hell out of this casino, call his wife, and tell her everything. She'd forgive him. He had a problem. He was sick. She'd have to forgive him.

He slid his credit card into the ATM.

ETHAN SAT on a stool in front of a slot machine he wasn't playing, sipping a flavorless free drink. He wanted to throw up. He had quit before his losses topped ten grand, so at least he had that tiny little speck of self-control...though he hadn't actually left the casino yet. There was still time to ruin his life even more.

He set the drink down, stood up, and slowly made his way toward the casino exit. Wherever that was. They didn't make it easy to find your way out. He'd call Jenny as soon as he left—he didn't think it would be good for her to listen to his confession with the chimes and music of slot machines playing in the background.

He could barely walk. He'd only had half a drink, though. At least he wasn't an alcoholic.

How the hell did he get out of this place? It was a frickin' maze.

"Hey," somebody said to him.

Ethan glanced over. It was a man, maybe thirty, immaculately groomed and nicely dressed in a dark grey suit. "Yeah?"

"Would you like to talk about it?"

"Not really." Ethan continued on his way, wherever that was. The man walked up next to him.

"I can fix your problem."

"What problem?"

"You look like you're sick to your stomach. You've got haunted eyes. It's not an uncommon look around these parts. You lost more than you can afford."

Ethan let out a snort. "You could say that."

"How much?"

"None of your business."

"Five hundred?"

"I wish."

"A thousand?"

"I said it's none of your business. I'm not interested in a high-interest loan, sorry."

"It's not a loan," said the man. "It's a game."

"I'm all out of gambling money."

"There's no buy-in."

"Then what's the scam?"

The man smiled and extended his hand. "My name's Rick Murray. I'm play-testing a game that could recoup all of your losses ten minutes from now. No financial risk to you whatsoever. You will not lose another penny. Maybe I misinterpreted your facial expression and body language, but you look like somebody who is truly desperate. Am I wrong?"

Ethan was silent for a moment. "No, you're not wrong."

"Then come with me."

"Where?"

"My office."

"I'm not going anywhere with you. This is becoming kind of creepy, so if you truly want to help me out, you can direct me to the exit of this funhouse. Otherwise, I'm not interested."

"Straight ahead, then left at the blackjack tables, keep going in that direction until you reach the wall, then take a right and go past the dollar slots until you see the exit to the left."

"Thanks."

"I'm not taking you down any dark alleys or luring you into a basement," said Rick. "It's a small office two buildings down. Totally safe. If I meant to do you harm, I wouldn't be standing here talking to you somewhere with cameras all over the place."

"Still, it's creepy. You have to admit that it's creepy, right?"

"I won't go so far as to use the word creepy. I will concede that it sounds like a scam. But I'll also say that if I were going to prey upon somebody, I'd go after a big winner, not somebody who just lost his life savings. You look emotionally destroyed. I wouldn't be able to squeeze any more money out of you."

"Then it's sex trafficking or something."

"I feel like any response to that could be taken as an unintentional insult."

"Like I said, I'm not interested. Thanks again for the directions."

"Not a problem. I hope everything works out for you."

Ethan started to walk away from him. Then he stopped.

If he was on high alert, if he didn't walk into a torture dungeon, if he didn't sign anything, if he didn't hand over any credit cards or identification...why not see what the guy was offering? Barring waking up in a bathtub with his kidneys missing, how could things get worse?

He turned back toward Rick. "Fine. Let's do this."

"Perfect. Follow me."

Ethan followed him out of the casino—his directions had been accurate—and out onto the sidewalk. They passed another casino, then arrived at the glass door of a place that looked like a fairly boring office building. He could see a front desk with a young receptionist seated behind a computer.

Rick pushed the door open and walked inside. This didn't look like the kind of place where people's organs were harvested and sold on the black market, so he went in after him.

"Hi, Mindy," Rick said to the receptionist as they walked by her desk. She grinned at him. Definite affection between them but they weren't sleeping together.

They walked across the small lobby. Rick opened another door, which led to an office that looked like a place where a low-level employee might sell insurance. As they went inside, Rick started to pull the door shut, then left it open. "Don't want you to feel uncomfortable," he said, sitting down behind the desk, which had a computer on it but little else. "Have a seat."

Ethan sat down on the chair in front of the desk.

"Can I get you anything?" Rick asked. "Water? Coffee?"

"I'm fine."

"May I ask your name?"

"Ethan Caustin."

"Pleased to meet, you, Ethan. I'll get right to it. I'm inviting you to participate in a game. After each round, you can decide if you want to keep going, or if you want to quit. If you quit, you get to keep your winnings. If you continue, the prizes get bigger and bigger. Now I need you to be frank with me. How much money have you lost today?"

Ethan saw no reason to lie. "Ninety-two hundred."

"And you don't have that much stuck between the couch cushions, do you? The loss hurts. I see that you're wearing a wedding band. How will your spouse take the news?"

"Not well."

"Newlyweds?"

"No. Five years." It was actually twelve. Ethan wasn't going to blab details of his personal life to some guy who might be trying to steal his identity.

"Any kids?"

"No." *Two.*

Rick nodded. "Let's call your losses an even ten thousand dollars. What if I told you that I could offer you a 99% chance of winning that money back?"

"I wouldn't believe you."

"Fair enough. I wouldn't believe me either. But that's exactly what I'm offering. In the first round of this game, you'll spin a wheel with one hundred numbers on it. If it lands on the numbers one through ninety-nine, I will immediately deposit ten thousand dollars into your bank account or, if you prefer, hand you an envelope full of cash. All of your anguish is erased, just like that. You'll walk out of here a new man. 99% chance. Forgive my unprofessional language, but those are pretty fucking good odds."

"And if I land on the wrong number?" Ethan asked.

"We break your arm."

"Excuse me?"

"We break your arm. Like I said, there's no financial risk on your part, but yes, if you spin the wheel and it lands on the number zero, we will break your arm."

Ethan pushed back his chair. "Well, screw that."

"Really? You won't risk a 1% chance of a broken arm for ten thousand dollars? Ethan, when I first saw you, you looked like you wanted to slash your wrists. You looked like you wanted to shove the barrel of a revolver into your mouth and blow your brains out. Isn't a broken arm better than having your brains splattered all over the wall of your hotel room?"

"Do you get paid extra for being so melodramatic?"

"I can't see into your mind or your heart, so maybe you're fine with the way things played out for you today. If so, you're welcome to leave. I hope you enjoy the rest of your time here in Las Vegas."

Ethan wasn't *quite* ready to leave. "How do I know it's fair?"

Rick stood up. "Let's go into the game room."

They left Rick's office and went into the room next door. It was bigger than the office but not by much. A brightly colored wheel of about three feet in diameter was mounted on the far wall. Next to it was a chair with a strange contraption on the armrest.

"That's our wheel," said Rick. "One hundred possible numbers. The one you don't want is zero, which you can see is dark red on a black background. The designer wanted to add a skull, but we overruled him. You spin the wheel. Anything but zero and you're instantly ten thousand dollars richer."

"How do I know the wheel isn't rigged?" Ethan asked.

"You mean with a magnet or something?"

"Yeah."

"I'm told that every single player we've brought in here has asked that. And the answer is: it's not, but we can't prove it, so we can make whatever accommodations you want. You can roll a pair of ten-sided dice. You can write the numbers zero through ninety-nine on slips of paper and draw one out of a hat. Any fair way you can think of to generate a random number, we can work with. We're not here to con you. I promise you will have a 99% chance of winning the money."

"Sounds too good to be true. How can you afford to give out that much cash?"

"We're extremely well-funded."

"How about this?" asked Ethan. "You write down a number. You fold it up and give it to me. I guess the number. If I'm right, I lose." He didn't see how they could manipulate that. Maybe a stage magician could figure out a way to do that trick, but they couldn't fake him out without any prep time.

"That would add an element of psychology to it," said Rick. "You wouldn't just pick a random number; you'd try to figure out what number I wouldn't write down. But for the first game, I'll allow it."

"You're very easygoing about this."

"We want you to win. It's no fun for anybody if you quit after the first round."

"Makes sense."

"Before you officially commit, I'll explain how the chair works. You'll sit down and place one of your arms—obviously, if you're right-handed we recommend choosing your left arm, and vice-versa—on the armrest. In the extremely unlikely event that you lose, I'll press a button, and that very heavy iron block will slam down onto your arm, hitting it right below the elbow. It will smash your forearm into that deep groove in the armrest, breaking it in at least two places."

Ethan stared at the armrest for a moment. "So it's a horrific arm-breaking."

"Oh, yes. It's not a hairline fracture. Your arm will be *broken.*"

"I don't think I'm interested."

"I'm not here to simply hand you free money. There's an element of risk involved." Rick walked over to the door and called outside. "Mindy? Could you bring me two of the introductory envelopes?"

Mindy stepped into the room and handed Rick two thick yellow envelopes. He thanked her and she left. Rick sat down in the arm-breaking chair and tore open one of the envelopes. He pulled out a large stack of twenty-dollar bills.

"Five thousand dollars," he said. "Our game is for ten thousand, so you'll get both of these if you win. Or, like I said, we can do direct deposit. Do you have a banking app on your phone?"

"Yeah."

"Good. You can verify that the money's there before you

leave. Do you feel like you have all the information necessary to make your decision?"

"I guess so, sure."

"Then I hate to do this to you, but it *is* a game, right? The offer expires in sixty seconds."

Damn. Ethan hadn't expected that. He didn't want to stagger out of here with a shattered arm from the Bone-Crushing Nightmare Machine. But there was only a 1% chance it would happen. A 99% chance that his problem would be solved. A 99% chance that he'd escape a devastating fight with Jenny. A 99% chance to chalk his gambling losses to a moment of weakness, and vow to never let it happen again. He'd get his note to himself tattooed onto his chest.

"Okay," he said. "I'm in."

"Glad to hear it." Rick stood up. "Looks like it's time for you to win some money. Have a seat."

2

"Do I have to sit in the chair now?" asked Ethan.

Rick nodded. "I believe that you and I have mutual trust. But in the same way that I don't expect you to trust that the wheel doesn't have a magnet that will draw it to a certain number, you can't expect me to trust that you won't make a run for it if you're unlucky."

Ethan wasn't comfortable with this. Yet he also had to agree that there was no way in hell he'd voluntarily put his arm underneath the iron block if he chose Rick's number. He'd flee for the exit, no question.

He sat down in the chair. He took a deep breath, then placed his left arm on the armrest.

Rick crouched down beside the chair and began to fasten some Velcro straps over Ethan's wrist.

"Whoa—hold on, is that necessary?"

"I can only speak for myself, but I would certainly pull my arm away."

"How do I know you won't set it off even if I win?"

"If you think that I'm the kind of depraved freak who would bring you here for the sick pleasure of breaking your arm, then I'll give you the opportunity to back out of our oral contract. I hope you'll play the game, but make no mistake—you're not the only person wandering around casinos with haunted eyes."

"Fine. Do the straps."

Rick fastened the straps. "And you still want to guess the number I write down, right?"

"Yes. Can we use my paper?" Ethan wasn't sure how they could scam him, but he wanted to take every possible precaution.

"Of course."

With his free hand, Ethan took out the note to himself. He handed it to Rick. "You can write it on the back of that."

Rick turned the note around without reading it. "May I use my own pen?"

"Sure. Actually, no. What's your receptionist's name? Mindy?" Ethan called out. "Hey, Mindy, could you come in here for a second?"

Mindy peeked her head into the room. "Yes, sir?"

"Could you get us a pen?"

"Of course."

Again, Ethan had no idea how they could scam him on this, but he wanted to take every element out of Rick's control that he possibly could.

Mindy returned a moment later. He thanked her as she handed him the pen. As she left, he looked the pen over very carefully. Just a regular ballpoint blue-ink pen. "Here you go," he said, giving it to Rick.

"Admirable display of caution," said Rick. "We've lucked out having you as a player."

Rick walked behind the chair. A moment later, he walked back into view and handed the note, folded into eighths, to Ethan.

"Guess the number," Rick said.

"Forty-nine."

Rick's face was expressionless. Ethan suddenly felt positively sick to his stomach. How could he have been so stupid? Of course it was a trick! People in Vegas didn't give you a 99% chance to win ten thousand dollars!

"Open it," said Rick.

Ethan unfolded the note. He had to use both hands for this, so if he saw the number 49 on there, he'd try to quickly unfasten the straps before Rick could make it to the button.

The number was forty-two.

"It's a *Hitchhiker's Guide to the Galaxy* reference," said Rick. "I almost did a *Clerks* reference and wrote down thirty-seven, or a 'Weird Al' Yankovic reference and went with twenty-seven. What thought process went into forty-nine?"

"Not much," Ethan admitted. "I just didn't think you'd pick forty-nine."

"And you were correct." Rick reached over and unfastened the straps. Ethan quickly moved his arm, as if Rick might suddenly change his mind and push the button.

Had he really won? When was the scam going to reveal itself? It couldn't possibly be this easy. Rick was going to tell him that it was actually ten thousand dollars off the cost of a timeshare condominium.

"Do you want the envelopes of cash, or an electronic deposit?"

Ethan didn't trust himself with ten thousand dollars in cash. He might end up right where he'd started. Or where he still was —this whole thing was so surreal that he couldn't quite process that he might have actually won the money. "Let's go with electronic."

"Do you have your banking information handy?"

"Can you use PayPal?"

"The service fee will come out of your payment."

"That's all right."

Rick called for Mindy again. Ethan gave her his e-mail address and she left.

"So would you really have pressed the button if I lost?" Ethan asked.

"Yes."

"You would've just sent me on my way with a shattered arm?"

Rick chuckled. "No. You would have received private treatment. People tend to ask questions when they see somebody staggering down the sidewalk shrieking in pain."

"Good treatment?"

"Not the best doctor, not the worst."

Ethan's phone vibrated. A new e-mail from PayPal notifying him that $9709.70 had been deposited into his account.

The e-mail had to be fake. It would be very easy to generate a phony PayPal notification.

He opened the PayPal app on his phone.

It wasn't a lie. The money was there. The game was real.

He just stared at his phone in a state of shock. His problem was solved. He wouldn't have to beg for Jenny's forgiveness. Ethan had envisioned a scenario where he literally threw himself down at her feet, sobbing, blubbering, promising that he'd do anything to make it better. His children would be watching, mortified by the sight of their father reduced to his lowest state.

Not anymore.

"Based on your expression, I'd say that the payment came through," said Rick.

Ethan nodded. "Thank you. This saved my life."

"I'm glad you enjoyed the first round of the game."

"There won't be a second round. I just crawled out of this hole and I'm not doing to dig another one. You said I could quit whenever I wanted."

"That is absolutely true. It's also true that me telling you about the second round does not obligate you to participate. If it doesn't sound appealing, tell me no, and we'll send you on your way."

"Fine," said Ethan. "What's Round Two?"

"The same basic game, but for fifty thousand dollars."

Okay, Rick had his attention. That was as much as Ethan made in a year. "What am I risking?"

"That's also the same. I'll strap your arm down and press the button if you lose. Essentially, the only change for Round Two is that you now have a 90% chance of winning."

Ethan said nothing.

"I don't know your financial situation," Rick admitted, "but I'm guessing that fifty thousand dollars is a pretty significant prize."

"You could say that."

"But there's a one in ten chance that you'll receive, as you described it, 'a horrific arm-breaking.' Still a pretty small chance. The odds are greatly in your favor. But when it comes to shattering the bones in your arm, a 10% chance is quite a bit different from a 1% chance. You now have sixty seconds to decide."

Damn. Fifty grand?

That could go straight into a college fund for Tim and Patrick. They were still eight and ten years away from that, so Ethan and Jenny weren't stressing over it quite yet, but it would be *incredible* to have that money there, waiting for them.

A 90% chance.

"Just to be clear," he said, "If I lose, I get the broken arm and I *don't* get the money, right?"

Rick smiled. "That's correct."

"Figured I'd check."

"I'm going to pause the sixty-second timer. Purely hypothetical question. If I changed the rules and said there's a 100% chance of you receiving both the money and the broken arm, would you take it?"

"Are you changing the rules?"

"No. Hypothetically."

"I don't know," said Ethan. "What if there was severe nerve damage and my arm never healed right? It sounds like it could be one of those things where the bones break right out through the skin."

"That's a definite possibility."

"That could mess me up for the rest of my life. I'm not sure I'd do it."

"I was just curious," said Rick. "We'll start your sixty seconds over."

Ethan wouldn't shatter his arm for fifty thousand dollars. But he was giving very strong consideration to taking a one-in-ten risk of shattering his arm for the money. He might regret this. He might *really* regret this. But it might also be one of the best decisions he ever made.

A 90% chance of not having to worry—well, having to worry less—about his children's future.

"Screw it. I don't need any more time. I'll do it."

"Oh, good. I thought you might be leaning in the other direction. Do you want to use the same method, or do you trust the wheel?"

"I don't trust the wheel," said Ethan. "No offense."

"No offense taken. I don't think my boss would like me using the 'guess my number' method again, since it's not truly random, but I'm empowered to make decisions like this, so if that's the way you'd like to play it, we can."

Ethan almost said yes, but he thought about the whole "element of psychology" thing that Rick had mentioned before. People who were skilled in that sort of thing could use subtle tricks to make you think they were mind readers. When the odds were down to one in ten, Ethan didn't want to take the risk that Rick might indeed make this less than random.

"No, I'll write down the numbers on pieces of paper."

Rick called for Mindy again, and she brought paper, scissors, and a green baseball cap.

"You can cut the squares, or you can pull out the number, but not both," said Rick. "You can write the numbers, but I'll need to verify that you didn't press harder on one than the others."

"You can make the slips of paper," said Ethan. He wasn't looking to beat the system.

Rick cut the paper into squares, then wrote the numbers zero through nine on them. He folded each number, then scooped them up and dropped them into the hat.

Without being told, Ethan sat down in the chair and placed his left arm on the armrest. Rick strapped his wrist down. He picked up the hat, shook it a few times, and offered it to Ethan. "Remember, you don't want to draw the zero."

As he had before, Ethan suddenly wondered what the hell he was thinking.

Was he insane?

How would he explain his mangled, useless arm to his family if he lost?

What if they had to amputate it?

What kind of idiot would agree to something like this?

"Can I still back out?" he asked.

Rick pulled the hat away. "Yes. Do you wish to?"

Ethan thought about it. Fifty thousand dollars. "No. Sorry. Just a quick moment of panic. Let's do it."

Rick held out the hat again.

Ethan pulled out a piece of paper.

He knew it was a zero. It felt like a zero.

Shit. Shit. Shit.

He unfolded the paper.

Eight.

Rick breathed a sigh of relief. "You looked so stressed out that it stressed me out, too." He unfastened the strap, and Ethan got out of the chair. Rick walked over to the doorway and called out "He won!" to Mindy. It was kind of amusing that a company that could afford sixty thousand dollars in prize money had Rick calling out to the receptionist instead of having an intercom system.

Ethan realized that he was covered in perspiration. It still wouldn't seem real, until—

His phone buzzed.

He'd received the payment.

"Congratulations," said Rick. "The odds were far in your favor but it took nerves of steel to go through with that. You are a true gamer. Can I get you anything before I explain Round Three? Water?"

"Water would be great."

After Mindy brought it, Ethan gulped down most of the bottle of water and resisted the urge to pour the rest over his head to cool himself down.

"Round Three," said Rick. "One hundred thousand dollars."

"Holy shit."

"You're right, holy shit. Exact same penalty if you lose. This time you'll have a seventy-five percent chance of winning. You'll choose from four slips of paper. Three of those slips will earn you a hundred thousand dollars. One will earn you a severely broken arm. Still pretty good odds."

"What are the actual betting odds on that?" Ethan asked.

"I'm not sure," Rick admitted. "I know that there are fraction, decimal, and American odds, but I'm not a big math guy. We'll keep it simple. Anyway, this time, I'm going to give you two minutes to think about it."

"I feel like maybe I should quit while I'm ahead," said Ethan.

"The choice is entirely yours. No peer pressure here. Except that I will say that the prize money is just going to keep going up. Let's return to our hypothetical discussion. Would you break your arm for a million dollars?"

"I don't know."

"It would involve a lot of pain and suffering, but I personally would go through a lot of pain and suffering for one million dollars. People break their arms all the time. People get limbs torn off in accidents. They aren't getting a million dollars for their misery unless there's a lawsuit involved. You see where the game is headed, right? Pretty soon, the hundred thousand may seem like chump change."

"How far are we into my two minutes?" Ethan asked.

"It doesn't matter. I'll be flexible."

If he excluded the first ten thousand dollars as recouping his gambling losses, he could leave here with a hundred and fifty thousand dollars. That was "pay off the house" money.

One in four chance.

Still favorable odds.

But "will almost definitely win" had transitioned to "will probably win." Probably. It was a pretty severe penalty to risk on "probably." And if he came home with a mangled, useless arm, it would basically ruin his whole announcement about the fifty thousand he'd won.

One hundred thousand dollars.

Seventy-five percent chance.

No. If he left now, he'd leave as a winner. He'd have only good news to share with his wife and children. They'd be thrilled when he told them. Would he regret passing up the chance to win even greater sums of money? Maybe. Not as much as he'd regret sitting in that chair with a huge metal block on his arm, gaping in horror at the visible broken bones, blood spurting all over the place.

He should quit.

He should absolutely quit.

But...

No. He should quit.

"I can't do it," he said. "If I stop now, it's been an entirely positive experience. I don't want to throw that away."

"Playing it safe, huh?" Rick seemed more amused than disappointed.

"Yeah. You understand, right?"

Rick laughed. "I was going to destroy your arm. Of course I understand."

"How high would the prizes have gone up?"

"Can't tell you. A lot, though. But you're leaving here sixty thousand dollars richer, so I can't imagine that you're filled with regret."

"Nope, I'm pretty happy."

"Let's make it official. Are you declining to participate in Round Three?"

One hundred thousand dollars...

"Yes."

Rick extended his hand. "It was a pleasure meeting you."

"The pleasure was all mine, I promise," said Ethan, shaking it.

"Doesn't it feel good to know that you can shake my hand without it jiggling the broken bones? Sorry—I try to keep the dark humor to a minimum, but sometimes I just can't help myself. I figure, it's funnier now than it would be if your arm had been crushed. Any plans for the money?"

"I think I'll—" Ethan almost said "put it in my sons' college fund," but he'd lied about not having kids, and he didn't want to end this on an awkward note. "—invest it. Maybe splurge a little, get a movie theater style popcorn popper, but I'll invest most of it. Gotta be responsible, right?"

"I totally agree."

3

Ethan sort of regretted not taking the envelopes of cash, because he could've poured the money out onto the bed in his hotel room and rolled around naked on it. It would probably be an overrated experience and result in paper cuts where he'd least enjoy them, but nevertheless, it was something he'd always wanted to try.

As soon as he'd left the building he'd transferred the money to his bank account. He handled all of the household finances, so Jenny wouldn't have to know that he'd lost and regained the ten thousand, but he'd have to figure out exactly how much of the truth he'd tell her about the fifty grand. He wanted to be as honest as possible...to a point. Now that he was away from the game, he realized that telling his wife that he'd willingly let a man strap his arm to a bone-breaking machine might create challenges in their marriage.

He wasn't going to outright lie about it. He would admit that he'd been gambling, and he'd explain that it was a cash prize from a game. He just didn't necessarily need to include every single detail of the experience. He had two more days in Vegas. There was plenty of time to figure out precisely how to share his exciting tale of adventure.

Now that he was back in his room, his plan was to call home, take a shower, watch some TV, and go to bed. If he'd won the money when he was young and single, this would have been a *very* different night, but though he was a piece of garbage who would recklessly gamble away money they most definitely couldn't afford, being unfaithful to his wife was not one of his flaws. No escorts for him.

"Hey," he said, when Jenny answered.

"Hey, you. How's the trip going?"

"Great. Really great. I can't wait to tell you about it."

"Well, I'm on the phone right now."

"What I meant was, the training sessions are going great, way better than I expected, but the details would bore the crap out of you. I can talk you through the whole day if you want, minute by minute."

"It's either that or I tell you about *my* day."

"Uh-oh."

"Let's just say that both of our sons have lost their video game privileges for a while."

"What'd they do?"

"I'll let them confess to you, one at a time."

"All right. Put the criminals on."

Tim had mouthed off to his mother, which was nothing unusual. Patrick had been caught trying to cheat on a math test, which was completely out of character. He'd cried when telling Ethan what he'd done, and Ethan felt guilty playing the role of

Stern Disappointed Father, considering that he'd expected to be begging for Jenny's forgiveness for his own mistake. Because Patrick was otherwise a great student—he'd cheated because he was worried that he might not get an A—the punishment from the teacher had been pretty light: three days of after-school detention and a zero on the test.

Ethan informed both of his sons that they'd discuss this when he got home. Then he told Jenny that he loved her and missed her. She said the same. He almost wanted to tease a big surprise, then decided against it. This surprise did come with a shameful confession, so it was better to do it in person.

He had tickets to a show the following night, but getting to the performance space involved walking through a casino, so he gave the tickets away.

When he got back home to Kansas City, he gave his sons their presents and their lectures.

He'd decided that he should tell Jenny about the money separately, so he waited until Tim and Patrick had gone to bed.

Ethan had a knot in his stomach as he took a couple of beers out of the refrigerator and handed one to Jenny. He honestly wasn't sure how she'd react.

"I have some news," he said, sitting down next to her on the couch. Their children had done sort of a mix-and-match with their parents' features: Patrick had Jenny's light brown hair but was unfortunate enough to look like his father in the face, while Tim had inherited Ethan's black hair but his mother's good looks.

"Good news or bad news?"

"Good news. Well, news with a very happy ending, and a bump along the way."

Jenny popped open the can of beer. "Am I going to need this?"

"It can't hurt."

She took a long swig of it. "Tell me."

"When I was in Vegas, I fell off the wagon."

"Oh, shit, Ethan, are you serious?"

"Yeah."

"I told you not to go on the trip. You promised it wouldn't be a problem."

"I know, I know. I should have listened to you. I was totally fine. And then I just thought, well, fifty bucks can't hurt, can it?"

"Of course it can. Didn't you have your note with you?"

Jenny looked like she was about to burst into tears. She seemed to have already forgotten that this story had a happy ending.

"I did. And I read it. I even read it out loud. It just didn't work. I started playing, and, yeah, I was down for a while. Way down. But in the end I came out ahead."

"How much ahead?"

"Brace yourself. Fifty thousand dollars."

"What?"

"I'm serious. We now have an extra fifty thousand dollars in the bank."

Jenny smiled, but then she frowned again. Her face

contorted as if she couldn't decide on which expression to use. "That's great! But...I'll be honest, I don't quite know how I should react to this. It's bad. You have an addiction. I'm happy about the money, but I don't know that I can be happy about..." She trailed off for a moment. "...the situation. Do you know what I mean?"

"I know exactly what you mean," said Ethan. "Regardless of how it turned out, I'm ashamed of this. I'm physically ill over it. It was a terrible error in judgment and I now know that I absolutely cannot be in that environment. I swear to you it will never happen again."

Jenny wiped a tear from her eye. "Okay."

"That said, I did win fifty thousand dollars."

"All in one jackpot?"

"It was a new game. Basically just spinning a wheel. The odds were overwhelmingly against me, but I got the big payout. I couldn't believe it. We can put this money into a college fund for Tim and Patrick, and even splurge with some of it. Go to Europe. Buy a TV that takes up an entire wall. Get some really expensive chocolates."

"No," said Jenny.

"No to the chocolates?"

"All of the money goes into savings. Every single penny. We should not be rewarding ourselves with a TV because you succumbed to your gambling addiction."

"You're right," said Ethan. "You're absolutely right. Put it in savings. That's what we'll do."

"Or maybe put most of it in savings and give part of it to charity."

"I'm all for that, too."

Jenny set her can of beer down on the coffee table, then leaned over and gave him a hug. "I'm sorry if I'm being a little bitchy about this."

"What? Are you kidding? No, no, no, not at all. You have every right to be furious."

"I'm not furious."

"Whatever negative emotion you're feeling about this is completely justified. I messed up in a big way. I could've just as easily come home and told you that we were fifty thousand dollars in debt. I put our family's future at risk. I'm completely appalled at what I did. Like I said, I promise it will never happen again."

"I believe you."

THEY DECIDED NOT to tell Tim or Patrick anything about this. The boys were way too young to be thinking seriously about college, so this was news that could wait until they were in high school. They didn't know about Ethan's problem, and Jenny couldn't see any benefit to saying, "Hey, your dad won big in Vegas while he was away!"

Jenny didn't bring it up the next day. She wasn't acting weird or anything, so Ethan thought he may have dodged a bullet. Thank God.

ON FRIDAY NIGHTS they went out for dinner, with each family member getting a turn at choosing the place. After some discussion, Ethan and Jenny decided that despite being punished, Patrick would not lose his turn. He always picked the same restaurant, so it was time for some delicious barbecue.

As Ethan squirted some of the spicy barbecue sauce on his ribs, he noticed Rick sitting by himself at a corner table.

What the hell was he doing here?

Rick was wearing a white dress shirt, with a dark blue jacket draped over his chair. He was eating his meal and not looking away from his plate.

Ethan suddenly lost his appetite.

"Is something wrong?" Jenny asked.

"No, no, everything's fine. One of my co-workers is here. I'm going to go say hi."

Ethan got up and walked across the dining room over to Rick's table. Rick remained focused on his dinner.

"Hi," said Ethan.

Rick glanced up at him. "Oh, hello, Ethan. This is quite a coincidence, isn't it?"

"What are you doing here?"

"I'm in town on business, so I thought I'd enjoy the famous Kansas City burnt ends." He took a bite. "They live up to their reputation."

Ethan pulled out the chair across from him and sat down. "Seriously, what are you doing here?"

"I'm sorry, did I not just answer that question?"

"Listen to me, asshole, I don't believe for one second that it's a coincidence that you're here. No way did you just happen to be in Kansas City for work, and just happen to be at the restaurant where I'm having dinner. Tell me why you're here."

Rick glanced across the restaurant, looking over Ethan's shoulder. "Is that your family?"

"None of your business."

"I thought you said you didn't have any kids."

"Those aren't my kids."

"Nephews? Stepchildren? Random kids you paid to have dinner with you?"

"I may not have been clear enough," said Ethan, leaning forward. "I want to know why you're here."

"My job takes me all over the country. I like to sample the best of the local cuisine. If we ran into each other in some low-rated dive, I'd understand your concern, but I'm at one of the most popular barbecue restaurants in the city, at the standard time that most people eat dinner. Personally, I was delighted that we ran into each other, but now you've ruined the moment."

"Bullshit."

"I thought we left on such good terms, Ethan. Why are you being so antagonistic? Your life is better for having met me, don't you think?"

"We didn't play Yahtzee. I was glad we met, but let's be real with each other, it was a sinister, fucked-up game and I want to know why you're here."

"You want full honesty from me?"

"Yes."

"The same kind of honesty you gave me about your children? How honest were you with your wife? Did you tell her the full story? Did you tell her how you were walking around the casino like a zombie?"

"I told her everything."

"Really? If I went over there and introduced myself, you're

saying that I could engage her in conversation about our experience without contradicting anything you might have told her?"

"Are you going to make me call the police?"

Rick blinked in surprise. "That's a bit extreme, don't you think? You're the one who interrupted my meal. I'm here in a public place. If you looked out your window in the middle of the night and saw me standing in your front yard, sure, you'd have every right to be concerned about your family's safety. But I'm here trying to enjoy some top-notch barbecue, and I don't appreciate you accusing me of stalking you. Call the police if you want. I'll show them my schedule of business meetings for tomorrow. I now regret choosing you. Sixty thousand dollars in prize money and you treat me like I'm lurking in your closet in a clown mask."

"Stay away from me," said Ethan.

"I didn't go near you."

Ethan returned to his table. His back had been to Jenny, but she'd obviously been able to tell that it was a tense conversation. Instead of trying to fake a smile, Ethan sat down, rolled his eyes, and sighed.

"What was that all about?" Jenny asked.

"Some jackass at work," Ethan said. "I'm having major headaches with the auditors because he didn't get me the paperwork on time."

"So you interrupted his dinner?"

"Yeah. No big deal. We worked it out."

"It doesn't seem appropriate to harass one of your co-workers while he's having dinner," said Jenny. "Couldn't that have waited until you were back in the office?"

She didn't believe him. Not at all. Excluding business trips, Ethan was very big on keeping his work life separate from his home life, and interrupting dinner with his family to go gripe at a co-worker was completely bizarre behavior. He'd have to acknowledge this or she wouldn't let it drop.

"It could have," Ethan admitted. "It absolutely could have. He just caused some serious problems for me, and he works from home most of the time. But you're right. It was inappropriate. I don't know what I was thinking."

"Maybe you should apologize to him," Jenny said.

Was she testing him? She had to be. She was trying to catch him in the lie. Shit.

"That's a good idea," he said. "I'll be right back."

He got up and returned to Rick's table. Rick, looking surprised, set down his fork with a piece of brisket still on it.

"My wife thinks I should apologize for disturbing your meal," said Ethan.

"Does she, now?"

"So I am apologizing for disturbing your meal. I hope you can find it in your heart to forgive me for my intrusion."

"I think I can get over it."

"Good." Ethan returned to his own table. "We're cool," he informed Jenny.

"Glad to hear it."

Did she believe him now? He couldn't tell. She might believe him, or she might have just decided to let it drop.

Rick left a few minutes later without looking at their table.

No way was him being here a coincidence. Not a chance in hell.

4

Jenny didn't mention it again. She seemed okay, as far as Ethan could tell. When he made a mild effort to initiate lovemaking, she wasn't receptive, but that wasn't necessarily a sign that anything was wrong. Twelve years into their marriage, he certainly wasn't batting a thousand in terms of getting laid.

Ethan had no idea what to do about Rick. He'd said nothing threatening, and "Don't you think it's weird that he showed up at the same restaurant?" wasn't enough for the police to take action. For now, he'd just have to be on high alert.

He didn't sleep very well.

He doubled his coffee intake in the morning and made it through the first half of his day at work. Sometimes he went out to lunch with co-workers, but today he'd brought a sack lunch, and since it was a nice day he decided to eat outside. There was a pond behind the building, so he sat down on the bench overlooking it.

Two bites into his ham sandwich, Rick sat down next to him.

"Hi, Ethan," he said.

"Hi."

"I suppose I'd be insulting your intelligence if I said this was a coincidence."

"Yeah."

"How's your sandwich?"

"It's kind of dry. What do you want from me? Are you trying to get your money back?"

"Absolutely not," said Rick. "You won that money. It's yours to keep. I'm just here to let you know that the game is still on."

"You said it was completely voluntary."

"Each round is voluntary. But the game goes on. Come on, Ethan, you don't look like a complete dumbass, so you can't possibly have thought I'd give you sixty thousand dollars and then disappear from your life. Of course I was going to show up again. But before you get too upset, it's not all bad. There are still prizes. And, again, if you don't like the odds of a certain round, you can pass. I think you'll have fun."

"You're going to make me call the police, aren't you?"

"Actually, that's why I'm here. There are two rules that you'll have to follow. The first one is, don't tell anybody about the game. That means your wife and kids, and it especially means, you guessed it, do not call the police. Don't call 911, don't contact the FBI, don't tell anybody. This game is our little secret. The second rule is, don't send your family away. You're going to think, oh, I'll ship the kids off to Grandma's until this all blows over, and I am telling you very specifically not to do that."

"You're saying to leave my family in danger?" Ethan asked.

"I'm saying that the money we used to hook you into this

game is a drop in the bucket. So you're putting your family *into* danger if you break the rule. I like you, Ethan, so I truly hope that you trust me when I say that you do not want to break this rule. This is as far from a bluff as you can get. I'd rather not get overly descriptive about the penalties, but I can if you'd like. Are we clear?"

Ethan wanted to punch him in the face, then drag him into the pond and hold his head underwater for a few minutes. Instead, he said, "Yeah. We're clear."

"So to recap: don't tell anybody, especially the police, and don't move your family. Now let me clarify Rule #1. *Nobody* is to call the police. If your wife Jenny, your twelve-year-old son Patrick, or your ten-year-old son Tim call the police, or if they alter their routine in any significant way, that counts as a violation of the rules."

Rick's lack of subtlety about knowing Ethan's family members was almost funny. "Anything else?"

"That covers it. We like to keep things simple. Good game design involves not bogging down the gameplay with unnecessary rules."

"Is it against the rules for me to call you a piece of shit?" asked Ethan.

Rick chuckled. "Verbal abuse is okay. Believe it or not, I'm on your side."

"Since you just finished threatening my family, yeah, it is kind of hard to believe."

"That's a necessary precaution. I want you to follow the rules, and I want you to do well in the game. I know this all sounds bad, but it may end up being the best thing to ever happen to you."

"I'm guessing it probably won't."

"Are you better off now than if you had to tell Jenny about the money you gambled away?"

"I'm not sure I am. Her life wouldn't be in danger."

"Her life is only in danger if she disobeys the very simple, very clear rules. She'll be fine. Your children will be fine. Don't be stupid. That's basically all there is to it. Don't give us a reason to carry out the threat."

"Fine," said Ethan. "I won't give you a reason to carry out the threat. You're still a piece of shit."

"We'll see if you still feel that way when this is all over."

"So what's the next game?"

"You'll find out soon enough. For now, just enjoy this lovely day, and I'm sorry that your sandwich didn't live up to your expectations."

Rick got up and walked away.

Ethan had no appetite now, so he put the half-eaten dry ham sandwich back into the bag.

He should've known something like this would happen. He'd been so desperate to recoup his losses that he'd played what was *obviously* the kind of game where evil people would show up to threaten his family. And now he was in deeper shit than when he was wandering around the casino, completely lost.

He wished he didn't believe that Rick would fulfill his threat if Ethan broke the rules.

He totally believed him. One hundred percent.

So there wasn't a damn thing he could do right now but play along.

"Did you see your co-worker today?" Jenny asked, as she broke a handful of dry spaghetti in half and dropped it into the boiling water.

This was definitely a test. Playing dumb by asking "Which co-worker?" would be the absolute wrong answer. "Yeah," he said. "I apologized again. I'm still pissed at him, though. When the auditors ask for paperwork, you give it to them. He had no excuse."

Ethan gave her a kiss on the neck, then reached over and stirred the spaghetti sauce, hoping she didn't suspect that he was lying his ass off. He was more of a "little white lies" husband—big lies like this were difficult for him.

Fifteen minutes later, Ethan had taken his first bite of garlic bread when his phone rang. The Caustin family had a very strict policy against using cell phones at the dinner table, so Ethan didn't take it out of his pocket.

After the call went to voice mail, it rang again.

After that call went to voice mail, his phone vibrated to notify him that he had a text message.

"I'm sorry," he said, taking his phone out of his pocket. "Somebody keeps calling."

The text message was from Rick Oddsmaker: *Answer your phone.*

"It's work," he said, getting up. "I have to take this."

Work calling him in the evening was completely unprecedented. He didn't have the kind of job where he was on call 24/7. He walked out of the dining room and into the living room as his phone began to ring again. He answered.

"Yeah?"

"Don't ignore my calls ever again," said Rick. "That's now the third rule: have your cell phone on and with you at all times. Should be easy to follow in a world where most people might as well have their phones surgically grafted to their hands."

"Sorry about that," Ethan said, trying to keep his voice casual. "I just sat down to dinner."

"I know. It smells delicious."

Ethan's grip on the phone tightened.

"I'm kidding," said Rick. "I can't smell the spaghetti."

"So what can I do for you?"

"I'm offering you a chance to win a bottle of Dom Perignon. 1970. I don't know much about champagne, but this goes for up to two thousand bucks, so it's probably pretty good stuff."

"Not interested."

"Well, Ethan, the rules of the game are that you can skip any round you want, but I do recommend that you hear me out first. Are you willing to hear me out?"

"Sure."

"There's a small playground six blocks from your home. A slide, a merry-go-round, a swing set with one of the swings broken. Do you know the one I'm talking about?"

"Yes."

"A couple of children are playing in the sandbox. I've calculated that you have a 75% chance of finding the three hypodermic needles that are buried in the sand before they do."

Ethan walked into the hallway and spoke in a whisper. "You son of a bitch."

"Think how much you'll enjoy that bottle of vintage bubbly. Pop it open after you win or save it for a special occasion—the choice is yours. Are you going to play this round? You have as long as you want to decide, but your odds obviously get worse and worse the longer they dig around in the sand."

"Yes, I'll play."

"Good luck to you." Rick hung up.

Ethan hurried back into the dining room. "I've got an emergency at work," he said. "I've gotta go."

"What kind of emergency?" asked Jenny.

"Auditing emergency. I'll explain everything when I get back."

"Ethan—"

He ignored her and headed for the front door.

As he drove toward the playground, he kept telling himself that this had to be a prank. No way were there really hypodermic needles buried in the sandbox. The truth had to be that Rick had a very dark sense of humor, and after revealing his joke and having a good laugh at Ethan's expense, he'd disappear from his life forever.

There were lots of little kids in his neighborhood, so he drove as fast as possible while remaining fully alert for children running into the street. He managed to make it to the playground without running anybody over. As he parked, he saw that two very young children, probably pre-school age, were vigorously digging around in the sandbox, while their mother sat on the bench that was right next to it, looking at her phone.

Ethan sprinted over to the sandbox. "Ma'am! I need your kids to get out of the sandbox right away."

"Why? What's wrong?"

"Somebody reported a hypodermic needle in the sand."

The mother immediately got up. She took the children's hands. "Let's go play somewhere else, okay?"

The kids stood up and walked out of the sandbox without protest.

Ethan used his foot to gently dig in the sand as the mother led her kids to the swings. A couple of older accompanied kids were sitting on the slide, not actually sliding on it, but aside from that the playground was vacant. After searching for a couple of minutes, he started to think that maybe it *was* a bluff, but then his toe struck something, buried about a foot deep.

As he carefully moved the sand away, it looked very much like the plunger of a hypodermic needle.

He pulled it out with his fingers. Yes. It was a goddamn hypodermic needle, filled with a light brown liquid.

Ethan kept searching. It took him about ten minutes to find the other two needles. They also had the same liquid in them. He didn't know his illegal drugs very well, so he guessed "heroin" but really had no idea.

He walked out of the sandbox with the needles. What the hell was he supposed to do with these?

The mother walked over to him. "Oh my God. Should we call the police?"

"Already done," said Ethan.

"I guess I can't take my kids here anymore."

Ethan would've loved to reassure her that this was a one-time thing, but he had no idea what that psycho Rick had planned for after this. "That might be a good idea for a while, until they get some people out here to thoroughly check for more needles."

Were there only three in the sandbox? Should he keep looking?

His phone rang. Rick.

"That's the police calling me back," said Ethan. "Sorry to have scared you."

"Oh, no, I'm so glad you warned me!"

Ethan walked back toward his car as he answered. "I found them."

"All three?"

"Yes."

"Congratulations. I knew you could do it. In the far corner of the playground, on the ground behind a tree, you'll find a small metal box. Put the needles in there so that they can be disposed of safely, and then immediately return home."

"What's in them?"

"Use your imagination. Are you headed toward the tree?"

"Now I am, yeah."

Ethan walked across the playground over to the tree. The small tin box was on the other side of it. He crouched down next to it, then hesitated.

"How do I know this isn't booby trapped?"

"Oh, for God's sake, Ethan, just put the needles in the box."

Ethan opened the lid. The box was empty. He put the hypodermic needles inside, replaced the lid, and stood back up. "I'm done."

"Go back to your car."

"What if a kid finds it?"

"They won't, if you go straight to your car and drive home."

Ethan decided that he didn't have much of a choice. He hurried back to his car, jogging now that he didn't have to worry about tripping and landing on the needles. He brushed the sand off his hands and pants, then got into the car.

"What the hell is the matter with you?" he demanded, after

he started the engine.

"What do you mean?" asked Rick.

"Don't play dumb with me. Those kids looked like they were three years old."

"I know. Adults don't usually play in sandboxes."

"What if I'd been too late?"

"You would've lost this round. No Dom Perignon for you."

"I mean it—stop playing dumb."

"Are you asking if somebody would have stopped those very young children from digging through the sand with their bare hands?"

"Yes," said Ethan.

"Absolutely not," said Rick. "That's the most important thing to understand about this game. There is no bluffing. If I say I'm going to shatter your arm, I will shatter your arm. If I say that children are in danger of jabbing themselves on a hypodermic needle, I mean it. Every single time I tell you the stakes, I promise you, they are real."

"This is so fucked up. When does it end?"

"I don't have a timeline for you. Hopefully it ends with your victory."

"You know, I had to rush out of the house during dinner. I never do that. I make everybody sit at the table with no outside distractions. So if you don't want me to tell anybody about what's happening, how about you not call when I'm having dinner with my family, okay?"

"I apologize for calling at a bad time," said Rick. "But guess what? That's part of the game. I'm not going to make it *easy* for you to keep this a secret, as you'll find out very soon. Anyway, go home. You have spaghetti waiting."

5

As he drove home, Ethan did a lot of deep breathing and tried to calm himself down, so that his lie of "Everything's fine!" would not be so transparent. He could see in the rearview mirror that his face was pale, but since he didn't have a makeup kit in the car there wasn't much he could do about that.

"Sorry about that," he said as he walked back inside. Jenny and the kids were still at the dinner table.

"What was wrong?" Jenny asked.

"Nothing. False alarm."

"Since when do they call you at home?"

"It's these auditors," said Ethan. "They don't have the usual boundaries. They're a complete pain in the butt. I'd tell them to knock it off, but, y'know, it's not a good idea to make the auditors mad."

"What are auditors?" asked Tim.

"They're mean people who spend all day trying to find your mistakes."

"Like my teacher?"

"No, Ms. Neary is trying to help you learn."

"Dad," said Patrick, "you tracked dirt through the living room."

Oh, shit. "Whoops." Ethan walked back to the front door and took off his shoes. The sand had all come off but he'd gotten dirt on his shoes running through the playground. Would that seem suspicious? It wasn't as if there weren't perfectly normal ways to get dirt on one's shoes that didn't involve sprinting through a playground after saving children from hypodermic needles hidden by a madman.

He returned to the table. Everybody else was almost finished with their meal. He swirled some spaghetti around on his fork and took a bite.

"What kind of false alarm?" Jenny asked.

Her tone seemed to be genuine curiosity and not "I know you're a lying piece of garbage." He couldn't blame her for not ignoring it. Getting a call from work and immediately rushing out of the house was simply not a thing that ever happened.

"There is something seriously wrong with this auditor," said Ethan. "When he wants something, he wants it now, and he doesn't care if everybody else has gone home for the day. He also left a message for Craig, and Craig got him what he needed. It's crazy. I may have to say something."

"Well, like you said, don't get the auditors mad at you," said Jenny. Did she believe him, or was she temporarily letting him off the hook? He couldn't quite tell. If it was the latter, he supposed he'd find out soon enough.

Normally the rule was that nobody left the table until everybody was done eating, but there were exceptions, and he couldn't very well make Tim and Patrick sit there and watch him finish when he'd been absent for most of the meal, so he released them. Jenny didn't leave.

"Are you okay?" she asked.

"Yeah, why?"

"You seem really stressed out."

"Audits are stressful. This one way more than usual."

"Sorry," she said, reaching out and taking his hand. "That sucks."

"It should be over soon."

"I hope so."

The doorbell rang. Ethan flinched.

"I'll get it!" Tim called out.

Ethan started to call out, no, he'd do it, but Tim was always the designated door answerer. If Ethan acted concerned about Tim answering the door, *that* would send up a huge red flag. It would be fine. It wasn't as if Rick would send somebody to grab his son as soon as he opened the door.

He was terrified, but he couldn't let this seem more unusual than it already did.

Tim opened the door.

He didn't speak to anybody.

He closed the door again.

Oh, God, did he go outside?

Tim walked into the dining room, holding a white cardboard box. "This came for you, Dad," he said, setting the box on the table.

It hadn't been mailed. It just said "To Ethan Caustin" in fancy black ink.

"What is it?" Tim asked.

"I'm not sure," said Ethan, even though he knew exactly what it was.

"Do you want me to get you some scissors?"

"No, hold on, let me finish my spaghetti first. I've got three more bites."

As he ate the rest of his dinner, he tried to think of a good cover story. The problem was that he didn't know what kind of note might be included in the box, if any. He wished he had the kind of living situation where he could open up a package like this in private, but that would never happen in his normal life. Jenny and the kids would want to know what was in the package that was dropped off on their front porch.

He finished his spaghetti and took the dirty dish to the sink. He opened a drawer, took out a pair of scissors, and returned to the table. "All right, let's see what we've got here."

He cut open the tape that held the flaps together, then opened the package. It was full of Styrofoam peanuts. He reached inside, suddenly scared that he might stab himself with a hypodermic needle, but found an envelope near the top.

Inside the envelope was a card. The front said, "Well played!" in festive multi-colored letters. The interior simply said, "Enjoy!"

"Any idea who it's from?" Jenny asked.

Ethan shook his head. He reached into the box until he touched glass. He removed the bottle, shook off the Styrofoam that clung to the side, then set it on the table.

It was indeed a bottle of Dom Perignon.

"Oh my God," said Jenny.

"Is it wine?" Tim asked.

"Champagne," said Jenny. "Very good champagne." She carefully picked up the bottle and checked the label. "Ethan, this is from 1970. Who could possibly be sending you 1970 Dom Perignon?"

"Is that a good year?"

"I don't know, but I guarantee you that a fifty-year-old bottle of Dom Perignon is insanely expensive."

"Maybe that was the year it tasted like shit."

Jenny set the bottle back down on the table and took out her phone. She tapped away at the screen.

Frickin' Rick. How was Ethan supposed to explain this? It wasn't a fair game if he made it impossible to come up with credible lies. There was no realistic scenario where somebody would send him a gift like this.

"1970 Dom Perignon Oenotheque...however it's pronounced," said Jenny. "750 milliliter bottle. I'm showing it here for $2399." She tapped away at her screen some more. "Looks like the average price is about two thousand dollars."

"Who would pay that much for a bottle of champagne?" Ethan asked.

"The real question is, who would send you that bottle?"

"I don't know. Maybe..." He started to say "the auditors" but that was such a far-fetched answer that it was best to not even suggest such a thing. He shrugged. "I really don't know."

"What do they mean by 'well played'?"

"It's probably not even real," said Ethan. "Somebody slapped a fancy label on a bottle of grocery store champagne."

"Why would they do that?"

"I don't know."

"All right," said Jenny. The obvious translation of her words was "We shall discuss this later, when our children aren't listening."

Ethan gently placed the bottle back in the box. He was far from a champagne aficionado, so this would be wasted on him. He also wasn't likely to drink a beverage that had been gifted to him by somebody who hid hypodermic needles in a sandbox.

"It's from the game you played in Vegas, right?" asked Jenny, after Ethan closed the bedroom door.

"I guess."

"Don't say you guess. It's the only possible explanation. You won fifty thousand dollars and they sent you this to congratulate you."

Ethan nodded. "Yeah, that sounds reasonable."

"No, it doesn't. Casinos don't send gifts to your home because you won big."

"I don't know what to tell you."

"The truth would be nice. You come home from Vegas with an extra fifty grand, and then suddenly you start getting phone calls where you have to rush right out of the house. Nobody has to bolt for the door because of an auditor's request. You've been acting tense and weird. I'd really like to know what's going on."

Was Rick listening to this conversation right now? How would he be doing it? Through their phones? Was the house bugged? Was it all a bluff?

Maybe it was a bluff. But Ethan couldn't take that risk.

"I'm sorry you don't believe me about the auditor, but it's the truth," he said. "I've never dealt with anybody like him before. If we don't pass the audit, my job could be at risk, so, yeah, I'm a little edgy right now. The champagne is probably from the people who run the game. They obviously have a lot of money at their disposal. This gift is a *good* thing, don't you think? When would we ever be able to get our hands on something like this? You should be excited."

Jenny stared at him, as if daring him to be the first to break eye contact. Finally she looked away. "I guess you're right."

ETHAN OPENED his eyes as his phone vibrated. He glanced over at the clock. It was exactly midnight.

He picked up the phone, turning it away from Jenny so the light from the screen wouldn't wake her up. It was from Rick, of course. Jenny was a very light sleeper, so Ethan was extremely careful as he got out of bed and walked into the living room. By then the call had gone to voice mail, so he called Rick back.

"You're supposed to answer my calls," said Rick.

"We were asleep," said Ethan in a whisper. "I can't just start talking to you while I'm in bed with my wife. What the hell am I supposed to tell her?"

"Relax," said Rick. "You called me right back so we're fine."

"What do you want?"

"What do you think I want?"

"I can't do this at midnight! I get that you think this is all part of the game, but you've got to be realistic. She already knows I'm lying. There's no way I can keep this up."

"Guess whose problem that *isn't?*"

"All I'm saying is that it's not sustainable."

"And all I'm saying is that keeping your family alive should be worth the effort of coming up with a decent cover story. Let her think you're having an affair."

"Who the hell would I be having an affair with who's sending me two thousand dollar bottles of champagne?"

"As much as I enjoy arguing with you, I should mention that your next challenge has a ticking clock element. Do you want to hear the prize?"

"What is it?"

"A point."

"What kind of point?"

"A point in the game."

"Well, that sounds delightful, Rick. I can't wait for the opportunity to win it. A point in the game. Wow." Ethan realized that he'd stopped whispering.

"Your odds aren't as good this time. I've calculated that you have a 50/50 chance of successfully completing this challenge. Do you know where Rendill Park is?"

"No," said Ethan.

"Look it up. A woman has been buried alive in a shallow grave. Find her before she suffocates. The supplies you need are in the trunk of your car. Good luck."

Rick hung up.

Ethan immediately called him back but Rick didn't answer.

Jenny would probably wake up when he opened the front door, but he couldn't squander any time having a conversation with her about this. He had to just go. If she woke up and discovered that he was gone, she'd call or text him.

He opened the door as quietly as possible, then ran out to the car. He unlocked the trunk and peered inside. A shovel and a flashlight. Jesus Christ.

After getting in the driver's seat, he pulled up Rendill Park on his GPS. Half an hour away. He started the engine and sped off.

Ethan hadn't even left his neighborhood before his phone rang. Jenny.

"Where are you going?" she demanded.

"I'll explain everything, I promise," he said. "I will answer every single question you have, but right now I need you to trust me."

"Just tell me where you're going, Ethan."

Rick had never actually set specific parameters for what he was allowed to tell her. Could he say he was going to Rendill Park, and simply refuse to say why? The idea that he was headed into the office at midnight because of an auditor's request was flat-out ridiculous, and he was better off not trying to make up a cover story.

But he didn't want her to show up at the park. He wouldn't tell her anything.

"I can't tell you," he said. "I know this is upsetting and scary, but I'm begging you to trust me. It's all going to be fine, and I swear that I'll tell you everything as soon as I can."

"Are you in danger?"

"No, not at all," he said, realizing that he might be lying immediately after swearing that he'd tell her everything.

"Fine." She was pissed. He wondered what she was envisioning. That he'd become a drug dealer?

"I love you," he told her.

"I'll see you whenever you get home," she said, and then hung up.

Ethan couldn't worry about repairing the damage to his marriage right now. He had a buried-alive woman to rescue.

6

Rendill Park had closed at dusk. The gate at the entrance wasn't one where he could just cut the padlock and swing it open. If he backed the car all the way to the road and floored the gas pedal, it was possible that he'd build up enough speed to smash right through it. Or, more likely, he might wreck his car.

He called Rick. No answer. He texted him: *Gate's closed. Am I supposed to be able to get through?*

A moment later, Rick texted back: *No help. You're on your own.*

Ethan got out of his car. The gate was a thick steel barrier (which seemed a bit excessive for a state park, but who knew what kind of mischief people got into after dark?) and he didn't see a way to drive past it. So he'd do this on foot.

He took the shovel and flashlight out of the trunk, then walked around the gate.

There was a straight paved road, long enough that Ethan

couldn't see the end of it with the flashlight beam. There was thin forest on each side of the road. Absolutely no clues about where a woman might be buried in a shallow grave.

He stepped off the road onto the right side and waved his flashlight beam around the ground. Presumably, he'd see some freshly overturned dirt to mark the spot. He didn't want to rush the process and miss something, so he carefully searched for a couple of minutes, then walked to the other side of the road and searched there as well.

Not a damn thing.

Was he supposed to search the whole park? Even in the daylight that would be an impossible task.

He had no idea what kind of time constraint he was under, except for the park re-opening at 9:00 AM. How long would it take her to run out of air? Even if he was familiar with this sort of scenario, which he was not, there were too many variables. A Google search for *How long does it take to suffocate when you've been buried alive* would not be useful.

Okay, the odds were a clue. Rick said he had a 50/50 chance of success. So the grave had to be close enough to give him a reasonable chance to find it. It wasn't buried at the end of the park, far off the beaten path. It was somewhere nearby, or at least there was a clue to its whereabouts. The game was evil but—thus far—fair, so he'd trust that this wasn't an impossible task.

The forest was thin, but the trees weren't so close together that a shallow grave could be hiding anywhere. If he assumed that she was lying flat on her back, and that they'd avoided digging through tree roots, he could at least narrow the search down to small clearings.

The forest went on what seemed like forever, but again, he

had a 50% chance here, so the grave had to be close to the road, right?

He continued searching, moving as quickly as possible while still being thorough.

The heavy shovel was slowing him down, so he lay it on the road.

Ethan really had no idea how far from the road he should look. Maybe the 50/50 odds were based on an inaccurate prediction of how he'd search. Maybe he was supposed to try to smash through the metal barrier with his car. He had no idea. This was insane.

For now, he'd stick with the plan. Search each side of the road, but not veer too far away from it.

How terrified was the woman?

Was she still conscious?

Was she clawing at the lid of a coffin?

Did she have a breathing tube protruding from the ground? Maybe that's what he was supposed to be looking for.

He kept searching.

ETHAN TOOK OUT HIS PHONE. He'd been looking for just over an hour. No new messages from Jenny. He wondered if she'd gone back to sleep, or if she was awake and worried out of her mind.

He couldn't think about that right now.

Rick hadn't said there was a penalty for bugging him, so Ethan called him again. No answer. He sent a text: *What am I missing? This is impossible!* No response.

He felt something on his hand and prayed it wasn't really a raindrop. He looked up, and a drop of water landed on his face.

No. No, no, no. It couldn't rain. That would erase the evidence of a fresh grave.

Just a couple of drops. No big deal. Nothing to panic over.

For the next fifteen minutes it was only the occasional raindrop, and then it started to rain for real.

He texted Rick: *It's raining! I can't find her if the dirt is wet! We have to cancel this round.*

This time, Rick texted him back: *Bad luck does not alter the rules.*

I no longer have a 50/50 chance. The odds have changed.

His phone rang.

"The odds are calculated when I notify you about a challenge," said Rick. "If they change, that's part of the game. If a park ranger catches you and kicks you out of the park, that also impacts your odds, but we don't give you a free pass for it. Stop whining and keep searching." He hung up.

Ethan didn't feel like he'd been whining, but now was not the time to protest. It was a moderate rain and not an all-out thunderstorm, so at least he had that going for him as he continued to search.

It was almost 2:30. Ethan was completely drenched and the ground was mud. It was possible that he'd walked right over her grave without realizing it. He had to hope that there was some other clue besides freshly overturned dirt, but he had yet to see anything even remotely helpful.

He wasn't sure how deep he was into the park. A mile? Mile and a half? His technique was to quickly search both sides of the road until the shovel, lying on the pavement, was almost out of view with the flashlight beam, then go back to retrieve it and start the process again.

Was he doing something wrong? Or had the rain turned it into a no-win game? He couldn't just start digging through random patches of mud.

Maybe his mistake was searching too thoroughly. Maybe he was just supposed to walk along the road, making good time, until he reached the obvious spot.

He decided to try that. Walking through the muck simply wasn't going to work.

Ethan had been walking for an hour. This goddamn park went on forever.

There'd been some decision points along the way. Three hiking trails. The primitive camping area. A playground. He'd checked out the camping area and the playground, but skipped the trails, deciding that they couldn't expect him to take a lengthy detour and have a 50% chance of finding her.

Unless they thought there was a 50% chance he'd take the detour. Fuck this game.

He was exhausted, but he couldn't take a break. He didn't know how long the woman had. If the difference between her life and death was the time he'd spent sitting on his ass, he'd never forgive himself.

Ethan went back to pick up the shovel. His legs collapsed

underneath him and he tumbled off the side of the road, splattering into the mud.

Fine. He'd take a one-minute break.

He just sat there, soaked and miserable, with the shovel on his lap.

He wanted to just lie back and go to sleep, perhaps drowning himself and ending this nightmare. Instead, he got up, then fell again, dropping the flashlight. He held it up to the rain to rinse off the lens, picked up the shovel, and suddenly noticed something.

Was there writing on the top edge of the shovel blade?

He held the flashlight right up to it. There was! Very small letters that said: *Look under the mat at the ranger's station.*

Holy shit!

He assumed this meant that another clue was hidden under the mat, but he finally had something to go on! He might be able to save her!

How the hell could they have expected him to inspect the shovel for clues? That was ridiculous. If this were a contained escape room, maybe, but not when he was supposed to be searching for a shallow grave in a state park.

Anyway, it didn't matter if the game was fair or not. He had to race all the way back to the park entrance, trying not to pass out along the way.

The surge of energy he felt from his breakthrough didn't last very long, and Ethan staggered along the wet road, slipping frequently. He moved as fast as he could, but the stitch in his side was like a knife jabbing him in the ribs, and he could barely feel his legs.

But he could do this. He wasn't going to let the woman die.

It felt like hours had passed before the park entrance came back into view. He lost his balance and tumbled forward onto the pavement. Pain shot through his face and he spat out some blood, though after a cursory check he didn't think he'd actually knocked out any of his teeth. He got back up and resumed running.

When he reached the ranger's station, he crouched down and lifted the doormat. A wet envelope was underneath. He tore it open and removed a piece of paper. The writing had smeared, but not so much that he couldn't read it.

Fifty paces ahead on the road. One hundred paces to the left. Dig.

Jesus Christ. If he'd paid more attention to the shovel, he could've found her hours ago.

He walked the fifty paces on the road, then stepped into the mud. One hundred paces were more difficult to calculate since he had to walk around trees. but this was far better than just randomly searching. The hundred paces took him beyond the area that he'd already checked. His current spot didn't seem right, but a few feet away there was a clearing large enough for a woman to be buried, so that's where he began to dig.

How deep was a shallow grave, anyway? Less than six feet deep, obviously, but how much less?

The wet ground was easy to dig. Two feet down, he struck something. Not metal or wood. Something softer.

It couldn't be an unprotected body. If they'd buried her like this, she would've been dead in minutes. He shone the flashlight beam where he'd made contact. It looked like cardboard.

Ethan frantically dug out some more mud, then crawled into the hole and used his hands to clear off the top of the cardboard.

It was wet but thick. With some effort, he managed to tear part of it open, hopefully giving the woman some much-needed oxygen.

"You're going to be okay," he assured her. "I'm going to get you out of there."

He tore the cardboard apart even more. By shining the flashlight beam into the large rip, he could see that there was indeed somebody underneath. She hadn't said anything.

Now the process was going faster. She'd been buried in what had probably originally been a very sturdy cardboard box. The woman was emaciated. Her mouth, partially open, revealed dark yellow teeth with a couple of them missing. She wore a ratty thin jacket.

Her hands were tied together at the wrists.

She wasn't moving.

Ethan tapped her face. It was cold. "Ma'am? Ma'am?"

No reaction.

He pressed two fingers against the side of her neck. Couldn't find a pulse.

Maybe he was doing it wrong. He didn't have anything to cut away the ropes, so he couldn't check her wrist. He stared at her face very carefully, watching for any sign of life.

There was none.

He held open her left eye. Again, no sign of life, but he wasn't a doctor and he'd never been this close to a potentially dead body, so he didn't know what to check for besides a pulse.

He pressed his fingers against her neck again.

Nothing.

He pulled her out of the makeshift coffin and dragged her out of the hole. He hadn't practiced CPR since high school, when performing mouth-to-mouth on the plastic dummy had been a great big joke for everybody, but he remembered the basics.

He blew two quick breaths into the woman's mouth, then pushed against the center of the woman's chest. Was it supposed to be ten times? Twenty? He'd go with ten.

Ten compressions. A breath. Ten more compressions. Another breath.

The woman was completely unresponsive.

He kept going, waiting for the moment where she coughed up some water and was suddenly perfectly okay.

Ethan lost track of how many times he blew into her mouth. He kept checking her pulse. Nothing.

She was dead.

Ethan let out a scream of frustration, not caring if anybody else was in the park to hear.

He should call the police.

No, he shouldn't. If they would bury a woman alive and let her suffocate, they'd make good on the threat to go after his family.

Yet maybe the police could actually protect them. Sure, he'd be the prime suspect in this woman's murder, but with forensics and DNA testing and all that, the truth would become evident. Even if they said, "I wonder if the $60,000 deposited into his PayPal account was for murderous services rendered?" he'd be able to somehow prove his side of the story, right?

He needed to get out of this game before things got even worse.

Should he call 911 or Rick? Or call Jenny and tell her to get everybody out of the house?

People might be watching the house. If Jenny and the kids fled, they could be in serious danger. So that was out. And if he called 911 and Rick found out before his family was safe, that might also be disastrous. He didn't know what kind of resources they had. Was it Rick and a receptionist, or something much bigger?

He needed to keep playing along until he could be sure Jenny, Patrick, and Tim would be okay.

He left the shovel and the woman behind and walked back onto the road, feeling dizzy.

When he got back to his car, his phone rang.

"Hello," said Rick.

"I found her," said Ethan. "She's still alive but only barely."

"Send me a video with proof that she's still alive."

What was he supposed to do? Jiggle the corpse?

"I'm already back in the car," he said.

"You left her behind?"

"I didn't want to risk hurting her more."

"C'mon, Ethan. Save the lies for your wife."

"All right. Fine. I found her. Fifty paces ahead and a hundred paces to the left. I was too late. She was dead."

Rick was silent for a very long moment.

"I guess you didn't earn the point, then," he finally said.

7

F*our hours earlier.*

The woman stood on the street corner, holding a cardboard sign that read "*Homeless. Hungry. God bless U.*" Rick rolled down his window as he approached and took a twenty-dollar bill out of his wallet. There were several cars behind him, so he couldn't have a full conversation with the woman, and he didn't want her getting into his car in front of witnesses, but he could entice her to speak with him further.

He pulled up beside her and handed her the bill. Her eyes didn't light up—she'd clearly been beaten down by life and couldn't summon any real happiness—but she did give him a crooked smile that was in desperate need of a dentist's attention.

"There's a fabric shop across the street," he said. "Meet me there and I'll pay you a lot more."

He drove through the intersection and parked in front of Tina & Mandy's Fabrics. In his rearview mirror, he saw the homeless woman crossing the street. She approached the vehicle on the driver's side, walking up to his window.

"Another twenty if you get in and talk to me," he said. "More if you accept my offer."

She shook her head. "I can talk here."

"I'm having a party. I want you to entertain my guests."

"What do I gotta do?"

"If you can't figure it out, you're not the right person. We'll get you a shower, a nice hot meal, and some fresh clothes. You'll feel like a new woman. Then you give me one hour of your time, making my guests feel good, and I'll pay you five hundred dollars."

"I ain't no whore."

"All right. Thank you for your time." Rick started to roll up the window.

"Wait. How many guests?"

"Three or four."

"One at a time or all at once?"

"One at a time."

The woman looked at the ground. "I don't know."

"Do you like drugs? I bet you enjoy drugs. What's your drug of choice? Actually, don't answer that. You'll probably say meth or crack, but I can get you the good stuff. I can give you some pills that will carry you through the whole experience, and then send some more back with you when you're done."

"What kind of pills?" she asked.

"You'll feel like you're floating. You'll barely know what's happening. You'll wake up with five hundred dollars in your pocket. No, six hundred. Plus the meal. What sounds good for dinner?"

"Steak?"

"Hell yeah, steak. I'll get you a great big Ribeye with all the fixings. Loaded baked potato, some freshly baked bread, and a side of your favorite veggie. How do you like your steak? I bet you're a medium rare lady."

"Well done."

"That's a crime against steak, but you're doing me a favor, so I'll allow it. Six hundred dollars, pills, an amazing dinner, a shower, and an hour that I actually think you'll enjoy. What do you say?"

"I don't know."

"Well, then I'll let you get back to your street corner. Buy something nice with the twenty bucks."

The woman sighed. "I'll do it."

"Perfect. Hop on in."

She walked around the front of the car and got in.

Rick handed her a folded stack of bills. "Three hundred up front," he said. "The other half when the party is over. Sound fair?"

"Yes."

"And here's a nice pill for you."

She tentatively took the pill from him, along with the bottle of water he offered, and swallowed it.

Rick started the engine. After he got back onto the street, he took out his phone and called Gavin. "I got one," he said.

"Will she be missed?" Gavin asked.

"No. Why would you even ask that?"

"It was a simple question."

"No, it was a stupid question." He glanced over at the woman, who looked like she was already having trouble staying awake. "Yes, I kidnapped the mayor's daughter and the entire Kansas City police force will be searching for her. I'll be lucky if there's not an APB for my car already. Her leg is hanging out of the trunk because I didn't close it all the way."

"You could've just said, no, she won't be missed."

"But then you wouldn't know what I thought of your stupid question."

"Who'd you pick up? Some crack whore?"

The woman was fully unconscious now.

"Nah," said Rick. "She's a homeless druggie but not a prostitute. Gross teeth. Whether she suffocates or we put a bullet in her head after she's rescued, nobody will miss her."

RICK PULLED INTO THE GARAGE. He waited until the automatic door had closed before he got out of the car. Gavin and Butch walked over and peered through the passenger side window.

"Ugh, you sure didn't pick a hottie. Did she stink up your car?" Gavin asked. As always, his black hair was slicked back with so much gel that Rick was surprised birds didn't get stuck in it.

"I brought some Lysol."

"Smart man. It's all about the advance planning. She's looking pretty emaciated and shit. I think Butch can carry her himself."

"Screw that," said Butch. He was an overweight guy who seemed to consciously dress to highlight this fact. Right now he was wearing a way-too-tight shirt with horizontal stripes.

"Why should we both get her reek all over us?" Gavin asked.

"Why should it be me instead of you?" Butch asked.

"Because you already have a below-average aroma. Sorry to have to break that to you. I'm sure you've always believed that you smell like freshly cut flowers."

"Just get her out of my car," said Rick. "I know you guys have nothing better to do than stand around and offer up witty banter, but I've got a schedule to keep."

"You think we're witty?" asked Gavin. "That's sweet. Thank you, Rick."

Gavin opened the door, and he and Butch lifted the woman out of Rick's car. "You wanna get the other door for us?" Butch asked.

Rick opened the door to the main part of the house. Gavin and Butch carried the woman inside. A moment later, Gavin stepped back into the garage, holding a shovel. "This is what's going in his trunk."

"Let me see it."

Gavin handed Rick the shovel. Rick flipped it upside down and looked at the blade. "The writing's too small."

"That's the agreed-upon size."

"He'll never see it."

"It's not like it's microscopic. It's totally readable."

"It's totally readable if he inspects the shovel. It's going to be pitch black out. He won't see it unless he shines the flashlight right on the words."

"I don't know what to tell you," said Gavin. "The rules are the same for everybody."

"Then let me add another clue. A piece of paper in the trunk. Not right out in the open, but something he'll find in a corner if he's paying attention."

"The tester found the message on the shovel."

"The tester knew to search for stuff like that. Look, I know that if I were in this situation, I would not be shining my flashlight beam all over the shovel in case somebody wrote a clue on it."

Gavin shrugged. "The decision has already been made. You're just going to have to live with it."

"Well, I disagree that it's 50/50 odds."

"Tough shit."

FIVE MINUTES TO MIDNIGHT. Rick tried to get into character. His call would be monitored, so he had to be a cold-hearted game master, the kind of sociopath who didn't care about Ethan's struggles in keeping this a secret from his family. It was, he supposed, all part of the game. Ethan needed ingenuity to succeed.

He didn't have a script, but he had key points to make, and he was most definitely not allowed to offer any additional clues. If the people listening to the call decided that he'd given Ethan too much information, they'd go into Termination Protocol, and that would be very, very bad.

He tried to channel his seventh grade math teacher, who had a zero tolerance policy for late work and who would mark you tardy if you showed up seconds after the bell rang. He couldn't let emotions play any part in this. He had to be impartial—though of course he was rooting for Ethan all the way—and heartless.

At midnight, he sent a text.

Ethan didn't immediately answer, so he called.

The call went to voice mail, so he called again. It was up to Rick to decide when to send somebody to deliver the message in person. That would, of course, be an absolute last resort.

Ethan answered.

"You're supposed to answer my calls," Rick told him.

"He's way past the spot," said Gavin, on the phone. He was inside the park, watching Ethan from a distance, only calling Rick with updates when it was completely safe to do so. "He's basically just going from one side to the other, maybe ten feet off the road."

"I told you he wasn't going to see the message on the shovel."

"Still plenty of time until dawn. You never know."

Butch was flying a drone far overhead, high enough that Ethan wouldn't hear it and he'd only see it if he decided to wave his flashlight around at the sky for some reason. The live camera feed wasn't particularly useful, but it let them track his location in case Gavin lost him.

"This is bullshit," said Rick. "I should be allowed to call him and give a hint."

"No hints for this one."

"I should be able to give him *something*. He's completely on the wrong track. He's never going to find her. What's the point?"

"Why don't I just walk over and take him by the hand? I could lead him right to her. I could dig her up for him so he doesn't have to strain his delicate fingers."

"Do you think she's even still alive?"

"Maybe," said Gavin.

"I bet she's already dead."

"If she woke up and started panicking, then yes, she's probably dead. If she's still asleep, or she woke up and decided to play it cool, she might still have some air left. How scared do you think she is if she's awake right now, huh? Waking up in total darkness, hands tied, not knowing where the hell she is, only barely able to move around...that's gotta be terrifying."

"You're sick."

"You love it."

"No, I don't. How about you only talk if you're giving me an update on Ethan's progress?"

"Sure, no problem. Right now he's getting colder, colder, colder with every step."

"THIS RAIN SUCKS," said Gavin. "Nothing like this was in the weather report. I'm gonna catch hypothermia out here."

"My heart aches for you," said Rick.

"Why are there no consequences for weathermen when they get it wrong? They don't know shit. They should have to issue a formal apology when they screw up like this. What other jobs are there where you can be wrong all the time and you don't even get reprimanded?"

"Should you be on your phone in the rain?" asked Rick.

"You just worry about yourself. I'll tell you what, though, they're sure as hell going to reimburse me for these shoes that are getting ruined."

"HEY, YOU WON'T BELIEVE THIS," said Butch. "He shined the flashlight on the shovel, then he took off back the way he came."

"He saw the message?" Rick asked.

"That's my guess."

"Maybe she's still alive."

"I wouldn't count on it. But you never know."

"If she never woke up, she might be breathing gently, and she might still have some air."

Butch chuckled. "Keep telling yourself that. Oh, shit, your boy just fell!"

"HE JUST LET OUT A LOUD-ASS SCREAM," said Gavin. "That's not a good sign."

"Nah, she's dead," said Butch. "He had the flashlight pointed at her when he set it down, so I saw every nasty detail. He did mouth-to-mouth and everything. Disgusting. I'm glad the camera is up so high, because if it was closer I'd be puking right now."

"I'm glad this is so entertaining for you guys," said Rick.

"I feel like you don't really mean that," said Gavin.

"Maybe Ethan enjoyed it," said Butch. "Maybe he slipped her the tongue."

"I'm going to call him. I've gotta hang up on you two idiots." Rick hung up on them and then called Ethan. "Hello," he said, keeping his voice neutral.

"I found her," said Ethan. "She's still alive but only barely."

Rick didn't mind the lie. He couldn't blame Ethan for trying. "Send me a video with proof that she's still alive."

"I'm already back in the car," said Ethan.

"You left her behind?"

"I didn't want to risk hurting her more."

Okay, now it was becoming a little insulting. He didn't mind the lie but he did mind the lack of respect for his intelligence. "C'mon, Ethan. Save the lies for your wife."

"All right. Fine. I found her. Fifty paces ahead and a hundred paces to the left. I was too late. She was dead."

Rick tried again to channel his seventh grade math teacher. "I guess you didn't earn the point, then."

"You're going to burn in hell for this," said Ethan.

"It's entirely possible. All right, this round is over. Leave the dead woman and go back home. I'll be in touch."

"What are you going to do with her?"

"Would you believe me if I said we were going to give her a respectful burial?"

"No."

"Then don't worry about it. You could have saved her but you didn't, so I hope you'll be more attentive to the small details next time." Rick honestly wasn't sure which fate would've been worse for the poor woman. Suffocating in a shallow grave, or being rescued from a nightmarish demise only to discover that she wasn't safe, after all. A bullet to the head was obviously preferable to suffocation, but having hope stolen away like that would be unbearably cruel.

"I'm going to kill you," said Ethan.

"That's fine," said Rick. "Go home."

8

Ethan was trembling as he got back into his car. It could've been from the cold, the anger, the horror, or all three.

He couldn't just keep playing along. What would the next round bring? A bomb for him to defuse before it blew up an elementary school? He'd failed a challenge already, and it was only the second one. They certainly weren't going to get easier or have lower stakes.

And what was he supposed to do when he got home? Keep a poker face? Tell Jenny that everything was perfectly okay, as his whole body shook and he tried not to burst into tears? At some point she'd demand that he give her the truth or she'd take the kids and leave, and Ethan had now been given absolute proof that they would kill people for this game.

He'd take it one problem at a time. Jenny first.

How closely were they spying on him? His phone conversation seemed to indicate that Rick didn't know that he'd found the woman and was too late to save her. But that was outdoors in a large state park. It didn't mean there weren't hidden cameras or microphones around his house. If they saw him whisper into Jenny's ear, they'd know he'd broken the rule. If they took a shower together, they'd be suspicious (or they might very well have a webcam in the shower). If he told her in the backyard, they might see her expression of horror and disbelief.

There had to be a way around it.

When could he tell her about the game without them knowing?

He had an idea. Probably not something he could make work when he got home, but later, if he could get Jenny to trust him.

He desperately needed her to trust him.

Half an hour after abandoning the dead woman, Ethan pulled into his driveway. If he was lucky, Jenny would be asleep. He'd sleep on the couch. In the morning, he'd say that it wasn't something they should discuss while he hurried to get ready for work. And then he'd have a reprieve until tomorrow afternoon. Technically *this* afternoon. His alarm was going to go off in an hour and a half.

Ethan was not lucky.

Jenny sat on the couch, eyes red and puffy from crying. Another trio of emotions flashed across her face: relief that he was home and safe, anger that he'd left, and confusion that he was wet and covered in mud.

"Where were you?" she asked, not getting up.

"A park."

"A *park?*"

Ethan nodded.

"What were you doing at a park all night? Why are you all dirty? Ethan, I need to know what's going on. We can't continue like this."

"I was working," he said.

"You were working," Jenny said, not phrasing it as a question.

"I have another job," he said. "Nothing illegal, I promise. Manual labor. Just to bridge the gap." He almost sat down next to her, but there was no sense adding "wet muddy clothes on the couch" to his list of infractions. "I lied to you about Vegas. I won big, yes, but I also lost big. I tried to hide it. I got a tip on this job that I thought I could do without you finding out, but I never imagined they'd call me at all hours of the night and demand that I get right out there."

"What kind of work?"

"Construction. I'm a contractor when they need somebody at the last minute. I'm sorry I didn't tell you. I was just embarrassed to be doing that kind of work. I didn't want you to think less of me for degrading myself like that."

Ethan looked directly into Jenny's eyes as he spoke.

Her father had been a construction worker, as had both of her grandfathers. Ethan had been a factory worker when they met, and then painted homes for several years. He'd been at his current desk job for less than two years, and occasionally talked about how he missed working outdoors. When Patrick, inspired by a friend, made fun of a grocery bagger, Ethan had shut that shit down *immediately*, making sure his son understood that there was no shame in an honest day's work.

The idea that Ethan would be ashamed of manual labor, rather than gambling losses, was so preposterous that he hoped it would send the message that she needed to just go along with this, and that all would be explained later.

Jenny looked utterly baffled.

Then she spoke. "Ethan, you never have to be ashamed. The work you do doesn't define you—you know that."

She was going along with it! Ethan couldn't believe it!

"I'll fix this," he said. "I'm just asking you to trust me."

"I trust you."

"Thank you. I'm sorry I lied. It will never happen again."

"I'd hug you," Jenny said, "but you're filthy."

"Right. I am. I'm going to take a shower. At this point I might as well not even bother trying to go to sleep, so maybe..." He lowered his voice. "...you'd be up for some makeup sex? Working so hard did something to me, I can't even explain it. We could go at it like wild animals, like we did at the cabin last year."

The cabin last year had incredibly thin walls. Ethan and Jenny had both been very much in the mood but had to be *extremely* careful not to traumatize their sons. It had been sex in super slow motion, with Ethan whispering dirty things into her ear the entire time.

"Okay," said Jenny.

Ethan took a very quick shower. When he stepped out of the bathroom, naked, Jenny was waiting in bed. He climbed into bed with her, dove under the covers, and went down on her.

"OOOOHHHHHH YEAH," said Butch.

Rick, Butch, and Gavin were in the van where they followed

all of Ethan's activity. It was Butch's turn to monitor the webcams in Ethan's home, but all three of them were watching at the moment.

"You think he knows we're watching?" asked Gavin. "You think he's a total exhibitionist?"

"Nah," said Butch. "They're under the covers."

"Yeah, but he's got to know we're watching."

"Maybe he thinks we're just listening."

"Maybe. It's still kinky."

Jenny's eyes were closed as she moaned softly in pleasure.

"We need that sheet to slide down a few inches," said Butch.

"You guys are perverts," Rick told them.

"I don't see you averting your eyes."

"Maybe it's a trick."

Gavin grinned. "Yeah. Maybe he's licking a message on her. I bet he's tapping away with his tongue in Morse code."

"I hope he can breathe under there," said Butch. "I'd hate to lose two people to suffocation in a row."

"You guys really need to grow up," said Rick, though he kept watching the monitor.

IT WAS difficult for Ethan to keep track of time down there. He wanted the show to start to get boring for the spectators, so he kept going, not adjusting his position.

"HE'S GOT some tongue endurance, I'll give him that," said Gavin.

"Maybe that should be one of the games," said Butch.

"How would it work?"

"I don't know. We find a really frigid bitch, and he has to finish her off within a certain timeframe."

"He's been down there for nine minutes," said Rick. "Is that really impressing you two? Is that a world record in the eyes of Gavin and Butch?"

"Hey, I don't go down there at all," said Gavin.

"That doesn't surprise me."

"It's emasculating."

"How the hell is it emasculating?" asked Rick. "Actually, don't answer that. I don't want to have that conversation with you."

"Bonnie pretty much makes me," said Butch. "She won't reciprocate otherwise."

"This is the worst porno ever," said Gavin. "I'm literally bored right now. Nothing here is going into the spank bank. I'm about to fall asleep right at the keyboard."

"Wait, wait, he's moving," said Butch.

"Oh, yeah, here we go!"

They watched for a few moments.

"Is he for real?" asked Butch. "They're seriously staying under the covers?"

"I'm telling you, he knows we're watching," said Rick.

"Missionary. For God's sake. Rick, can't you call him and tell him to get some doggy-style action going or something?"

"Sorry."

"Sounds like she's enjoying it, at least," said Gavin.

"Well, I'm not," said Butch. "This is bullshit."

JENNY MOANED WITH ECSTASY, even though Ethan wasn't actually inside her.

He was too stressed out to get hard. After mounting her, he began vigorously thrusting away, hoping she'd know not to say anything. She played along, even though she had to be utterly bewildered by what was going on.

He kissed her neck as he pretended to pound into her.

GAVIN WAS NO LONGER WATCHING. Butch continued to watch but looked annoyed.

"They could at least vary it up a little," said Butch.

"Maybe they're not exhibitionists," said Rick. "They could just be a happy couple making sweet love."

"Yeah, yeah, kudos to them."

ETHAN LICKED JENNY'S EARLOBE.

"Keep doing what you're doing," he whispered. Unless there was a webcam mounted right in the pillow, they wouldn't be able to see his lips move.

Jenny continued to moan.

"It's a game," he whispered. "I thought it was over in Vegas but it's not. They're forcing me to keep playing. When I get those calls and leave the house, it's for the next challenge."

He wished he could see her face, to make sure she wasn't giving anything away. But if she was faking sexual pleasure, the shock might not be recognizable on her face, if they could even see her face.

She hadn't stopped moaning. She was still playing along.

He licked her neck then returned to her ear. "I'm not allowed to tell you. We're not allowed to call the police. If you break the rules, we're in danger."

"I CAN'T BELIEVE he's still going like that," said Butch. "I think our little player had himself a dose of Viagra."

"Maybe," said Rick.

"What's wrong?"

"I don't like that his mouth is right up against her ear."

"He's nibbling her earlobe. I do that to Bonnie sometimes if I'm feeling all tender and shit. You think he's whispering to her?"

"He could be."

"What do you think? Sweet nothings? Nasty stuff? Or do you think he's telling her about the game?"

Rick leaned closer to the monitor. "I'm not sure. I don't like it."

"Do you want to terminate his game?"

"No. It might be nothing."

"He might be saying how much he likes to fuck her."

On the monitor, Ethan kissed Jenny on the mouth.

"We'll switch to enhanced surveillance on the wife," said

Rick. "Any indication that she knows the deal, and we'll do a full cleanup."

"At least they got laid one last time," said Butch.

ETHAN MOANED, shuddered, and pretended to have an orgasm, the first time he'd ever had to fake it. Then he and Jenny just held each other.

He assumed she was freaking out on the inside, but as long as she stopped questioning his activities, that was one big step toward escaping from this nightmare.

Hopefully he'd never have to tell her about the dead woman.

Hopefully there wouldn't be any more dead women.

9

Ethan's job required a lot of focus and attention to detail, which wasn't ideal when he'd had less than two hours of sleep the previous night. He tried to compensate for it with a massive amount of caffeine, but so far the cups of coffee weren't helping much. With everything else that was going on in his life, he couldn't afford to get written up for falling asleep at his desk, so he fought through it.

He kept waiting for a call from Rick, forcing him to make up some sort of excuse to leave work early, but his phone remained silent.

When he got home after an unproductive day at the office, he napped on his recliner for about half an hour until Jenny got home. She asked him about his day, and told him about hers, and though he could sense the underlying tension, she wasn't behaving in an manner that would seem suspicious to anybody who might be watching or listening. She was actually a pretty remarkable actor.

He made it through dinner with the family (baked chicken) without falling asleep. He tried to help Tim with his homework but offered no useful assistance, and then fell asleep on the couch as everybody watched television. At ten o'clock, Jenny prodded him to say it was time for bed. He could barely keep awake to get undressed, and was asleep almost immediately after getting under the covers.

He woke up at midnight.

He picked up his phone. No missed calls or texts.

Rick had given him no timeframe for the next round. He'd assumed it would happen pretty quickly, but that wasn't based on anything Rick had actually said.

Ethan tried to go back to sleep. He couldn't.

Dammit.

He lay there, waiting for the phone to vibrate and praying that it didn't.

Get some more sleep. You may need it.

Now he was wide awake.

He just lay there.

After a while, he wanted to give up and get out of bed, but if he woke Jenny up she'd think it was related to the game and she'd worry. If he had to scare his wife, he at least wanted it to be when there was legitimate reason to be afraid.

He tried various tricks to fall asleep, but none of them worked. This wasn't fair.

He finally drifted back off to sleep just in time to be tired as hell when the alarm went off.

He went with energy drinks instead of coffee at work, though they didn't seem to work any better. He really hoped Rick didn't call, because unless the challenge involved losing consciousness, he was screwed.

Rick didn't call.

When he got home, Ethan napped for an hour and felt a little better. He'd thought about stopping by a pharmacy for some sleep aids, but what if Rick contacted him while he was dosed up? More people could die.

At six o'clock, while Jenny was making dinner, he called.

"Hello," said Ethan.

"Hello. Did you enjoy your day off?"

"Yes, it was very relaxing."

"Well, it's time for the next round. Report immediately to the strip mall on 237 Weston Highway."

"What's the challenge?"

"You'll be told when you arrive."

"Hold on, that's not how this works," said Ethan. Jenny was staring at him, so he lowered the phone. "It's work," he told her. She immediately turned her focus back to preparing dinner. Ethan walked back into his bedroom. "What are my odds?"

"You'll find that out when you're told about the challenge."

"Tell me now. I'm allowed to say no, right?"

"That's right."

"And what happens then?"

"Things proceed the way they would if you didn't participate."

"So you're saying that you would've—" Ethan lowered his voice to a whisper "—buried the woman alive even if I declined?"

"Correct."

"Then I don't really have a choice, do I?"

"You still have free will, Ethan. It's not my fault if you have a conscience."

"You're a piece of shit. Have I told you that today?"

"Not today. So I can expect to see you at 237 Weston Highway, departing immediately?"

"Yeah."

Rick hung up. Ethan cursed and walked back into the kitchen. Jenny looked over at him, not doing a very good job of hiding her concern. "Do you have to go in to work?" she asked.

Ethan nodded.

"For how long?"

"I don't know. For however long they need me. I'll call when I know more."

"All right."

"I'm sorry to miss dinner. It smells delicious."

"I'll leave a plate in the refrigerator."

Ethan walked over and gave her a kiss on the cheek. He wanted to whisper something reassuring to her, but that would be too risky.

"I have to go in to work," he told Patrick and Tim, who were in the living room playing a gory video game. "Don't eat all of the tuna noodle casserole."

"We won't," said Tim.

"Why do you have to go back to work?" asked Patrick.

"Things are crazy there right now. It shouldn't last much longer." On the screen, a barbarian decapitated an armored knight in a cartoonishly large spray of blood. "Did your mom buy you that game?"

"No, you did."

"We'll talk about this when I get back," he said.

Ethan drove to the strip mall, which had a couple of restaurants, a nail salon, a tax service, and a party supplies shop. He parked in front of the nail salon and waited for Rick to call.

Instead, Rick walked up to his car. He knocked on the window, then opened the door and slid into the passenger seat.

"I get to see you in person this time," said Ethan. "What an honor."

"Don't get used to it."

"What's the challenge?"

"Stop being so impatient," said Rick. "We'll get to it. There's something I want to discuss with you first."

"Okay."

"You know we're monitoring you, right? That's no surprise. We wouldn't set the rules if we couldn't verify that you were following them."

"I assumed you were listening in, yeah."

"And watching."

"Oh. I didn't know you were watching."

"I made it clear that I was when I made the comment about you having spaghetti for dinner. 'I can see you' is exactly the message I was trying to convey."

"Sorry. This is about last night, right?"

"Yes."

"Sorry. I thought that make-up sex would keep her from asking more questions. I apologize if you're mentally scarred by what you saw."

"We didn't see anything. You kept it under the covers."

"I hope you're not asking me to ditch the covers next time."

"No, Ethan, I am not."

"I didn't realize there was a no-sex rule in place. You said to behave the way we normally do, and normally we do what married couples do. Now that I know you're being a Peeping Tom I obviously won't do it again. I'm just glad you saw a halfway decent performance."

Rick stared at him for a moment. "I'm not sure if you actually think this is about me being a prude, or if you're faking it."

"I assumed it made you uncomfortable to watch us bone."

"I could've looked away. I could've turned the volume down."

"I wish you had. No offense, but you watching my wife and I make love is a little creepy."

"You're pretty casual with the banter, considering that a woman died a horrible death two nights ago. Suffocation is a terrible way to go. I can't imagine how much she suffered."

"Keeping it casual is how I'm saving myself from a complete mental breakdown," said Ethan. "You're not good at subtly guiding a conversation, so if you're not here to tell me my next challenge, tell me why you're in my car."

"What were you whispering into Jenny's ear?"

"When?"

"When you were fucking her."

"I wasn't whispering anything."

"I saw you."

"I nibbled on her earlobe. It turns her on."

"And then you whispered."

"If I did whisper, it was filthy gibberish. I didn't whisper an actual sentence. I don't think I formed real words. I may have gasped into her ear. I don't know."

"You don't remember?" asked Rick.

"No."

"Hmmm."

"Look, I'm sure that when you have sex with your wife or girlfriend or friend with benefits you take careful notes to remind you of everything that happened, but when *I'm* in the throes of passion, I like to lose myself in the moment. It's obvious what you're trying to accuse me of, but that's just not what happened."

"Hmmm."

"Stop hmmm-ing at me. I didn't tell her a thing. You think I'd put my wife and kids at risk like that? Are you seriously saying that I would come home after you proved that you're the kind of psychopath who would tie up a woman and bury her alive, and then I'd immediately break your rule about not telling anybody about this? Do you think I'm insane?"

Rick said nothing.

"Do you keep the videos? Do you have a way to zoom in? Because I swear to you, I'm following the rules."

"All right," said Rick. "I'll let it drop. But don't give me a reason to doubt you again."

"I won't nibble anywhere near her ear."

"Good."

"By the way, which is it? Wife, girlfriend, or friend with benefits?"

"That's none of your business."

"Sorry," said Ethan. "I figured that since you watched me bang my wife it was okay for me to ask about your relationship status."

"Would you like to hear your next challenge?"

"Yes."

"The odds are 50/50 again."

"Because that worked out so great last time."

"The odds were accurate. We calculated that there was a fifty percent chance that you'd inspect the shovel."

"How do you calculate something like that? It feels like the kind of numbers that one might pull out of one's ass."

Rick frowned. "I remember giving you permission to be verbally abusive, but that doesn't mean it doesn't piss me off. If you want to be sarcastic, go right ahead, but I'm not sure how that improves your situation. Why be antagonistic? What do you gain?"

"You're right," said Ethan. "I apologize. I guess I just get testy when...you know what, I was going to make a sarcastic comment and I won't. So I apologize."

"Here's your challenge. An elderly woman lives alone in an isolated farmhouse. She's mostly bedridden. Her caregiver has gone home for the night. A man is going to break into her home to slash her throat with a hunting knife. Your task is to stop him."

Ethan stared at Rick. "Oh my God."

"I have faith in you. Technically you only have a 50% chance of succeeding, but I believe you'll do it."

"That makes me feel so very...nope, sorry, I was going to be sarcastic again. If you say you're my ally in this, I'll trust you."

Rick smiled. "Hard as it is to believe, it's true."

"What's the woman's address?"

Rick took out his phone and glanced at the screen. "I can tell you in six minutes."

"So we're just going to sit here and make awkward conversation until then?"

"It doesn't have to be awkward."

"I guess we could play word games or something. Oh, wait, you didn't tell me what glorious prize I'll receive if I save the woman from the psycho killer."

"A point."

"You guys are getting cheap," said Ethan. "You go from two thousand dollar champagne to a point."

"I assure you, the point is more valuable than the Dom Perignon."

"So do you enjoy doing this to me?"

Rick considered that. "I enjoy parts of it."

"Do you enjoy the 'suffocate an innocent woman in a shallow grave' part?"

"No."

"What about the part where an old lady might get her throat slit?"

"No."

"So what do you enjoy?"

"I enjoy setting up the game. I wish the stakes were different."

"They don't have to be like this. You could run a Dungeons & Dragons campaign. Your players would only die from their bad eating habits."

"I'd rather not talk anymore, if it's all right with you," said Rick.

Ethan shrugged. "You're the boss. Obviously."

A few minutes later, Rick said, "Do you have your GPS ready?"

"Yes."

"Put in 1010 Harwind Way."

Ethan put it in. "Twenty-three minutes away."

"I'd try to get there faster." Rick opened the door. "Good luck. I hope you save her."

10

Ethan sped down the highway, cursing frequently.

He'd asked Rick one last question: If he got pulled over for speeding, did that count as contacting the police? Rick looked surprised by the question, as if he hadn't considered that, and after a moment of thought said that, yes, getting pulled over by the cops would count as breaking the rule.

So Ethan was driving fast, but not *too* fast.

Why hadn't he listened to the message in his note? He'd carried that note to himself in his wallet for years to prevent him from gambling, and he still went ahead and threw money into slot machines, and now look what was happening to him.

Right now you'd give anything to be able to take it all back. YOU ARE MISERABLE.

Rick had strapped his arm into a bone-breaking machine. Why had Ethan gone through with that? He should have said to himself, "*Hey, y'know, if they've got this contraption set up to shatter your arm, perhaps these aren't the kind of individuals to involve yourself with.*" The arm-breaking machine was a gigantic fucking red flag! How could he have been so stupid?

Why did he even go on the business trip? He had no business being in Vegas. He should've known how weak-willed he could be. When Jenny said that maybe it wasn't the best idea for him to go, he should have agreed with her and stayed the hell home. Right now he'd be at home eating tuna noodle casserole instead of driving to rescue a woman from a knife-wielding maniac.

Weirdly, it hadn't occurred to him until this very moment that he might also end up on the receiving end of this knife. He could die tonight.

He had a wife and kids. Maybe he should decline to participate in this round.

No. He wasn't going to let a woman die. *Another* woman die.

He could do this.

He saw the farmhouse up ahead. Rick had been right: it was definitely isolated. Somebody could scream bloody murder as a hunting knife slammed repeatedly into their flesh and no neighbors would hear.

He pulled into the driveway. There was only one other car. Did it belong to the woman who lived there, or the man trying to kill her?

Ethan shut off his car and got out. He hurried over to the front door and tested the knob.

Unlocked.

He went inside.

The house was dark and quiet. No sounds of a murder in progress.

"Hello?" he called out.

No answer.

He walked through the living room. Lots of clutter and dust. He stepped into a short hallway with three closed doors.

He opened the door at the end, which led to a bathroom.

The door on the right led to a bedroom, but it was empty, and nobody appeared to have slept there recently. No blood on the blankets.

The door on the left led to an office.

Ethan returned to the living room and hurried up the stairs.

Two more closed doors.

He opened the first one. A small bedroom. An old woman lay on the bed, under the blankets, eyes closed. She looked peaceful. A moment of observation showed that she was breathing.

Was this it? Had he won?

Downstairs, he heard the front door open.

He didn't want to confront a madman with a knife head-on. He needed to surprise him. Ethan stood there, listening for the sound of creaking stairs, but didn't hear it. It sounded like the intruder had gone into the downstairs hallway instead.

Ethan rapidly but quietly stepped out of the bedroom and opened the other door, which led to a bathroom. He went inside, leaving the door open for now.

He needed a weapon.

At a quick glance, this bathroom seemed woefully lacking in weapons. A toilet plunger probably wouldn't do the trick. A nice jagged shard of glass from the medicine cabinet mirror would be helpful, but he didn't want to make noise by breaking it.

There was a hair dryer. Better than nothing.

He slowly closed the bathroom door just enough that he could hide behind it, while somebody glancing over would see that it was an empty bathroom and hopefully not bother searching for a victim. He angled the medicine cabinet door so that he could see the hallway in the mirror.

He waited. He was definitely breathing too loud, so he focused on keeping it under control.

He couldn't believe he was doing this. This was insane.

The stairs began to creak.

Now Ethan stopped breathing altogether.

The man reached the top of the stairs. He was a big guy, wearing jeans and a red-and-white plaid shirt. The knife in his hand was no joke. Eight inches at least. Ethan's heart gave a jolt as the man glanced over at the bathroom.

Then he looked over at the bedroom.

And then back at the bathroom. Shit. Did he know somebody was in the house, trying to stop him?

He held the knife out in front of him and walked toward the bathroom.

Then he stopped.

He looked like he was having trouble figuring out what to do.

He turned around and raced toward the bedroom.

Ethan ran out of the bathroom and chased after him.

Apparently Ethan was the better sprinter. He reached the man just as he stepped through the doorway. He swung the hair dryer at him, aiming for the back of his head but bashing it into his spine instead.

The hair dryer popped out of Ethan's hand.

The man stumbled forward, then spun around to face him.

He charged at Ethan, knife raised.

Ethan took a couple of steps backward, holding up his hands

as if that would somehow defend him from an eight-inch hunting knife.

The man accidentally bashed his knife-holding hand against the doorway as he tried to run through it.

It was a slapsticky moment that would have been hilarious if Ethan had been watching it on a YouTube video and somebody else was the target. It also would've been funnier if the man dropped his knife, which he most certainly did not.

A flash of embarrassment crossed his face. It immediately turned to anger.

He charged at Ethan again.

Ethan took another step back and smacked into the wall. The man tried to slam the knife into his face and struck the wall where Ethan's head had been only an instant earlier. The blade only went in about an inch, but it was enough for it to stick for a moment, as Ethan tackled him.

The knife, sadly, came free of the wall and stayed in the man's hands as both of them fell to the floor.

"Who's there?" the woman cried out.

Ethan cried out himself as the man slashed him across the arm, cutting him from the top of the wrist to halfway up his forearm. Ethan punched him in the face. The man punched him back. The man's punch had much more impact, and Ethan's vision went black for a second. It was the first time in his adult life that he'd been punched in the face. The other time, as a kid, had been by a bully wearing mittens in the winter. This was infinitely more painful.

The man got up.

Ethan grabbed his leg.

"Who's there?" the woman shouted again. "I have a gun!"

Rick had never said she *didn't* have a gun. If she opened fire, would she know which of them was the bad guy?

The man tried to kick Ethan's hand away with his free foot. He wobbled, almost losing his balance, but regained his center of gravity right away. The man was in a pretty good position to stab Ethan in the head, so Ethan let go of his leg and got up. He tackled him again, praying he wouldn't get stabbed in the process.

"*Who's in my home?*" the woman shrieked. She had yet to get out of bed and point a shotgun at them, so that was a plus, at least.

Ethan and the man struck the wall, struck the opposite wall, then veered way too close to the top of the stairs.

Ethan's leg twisted out from under him and he fell, taking the man with him as they crashed onto the staircase and tumbled down a few steps. The man got the worst of it, until Ethan smacked his head.

He tried to snap his vision back into focus before the man slashed his throat.

Instead of murdering him, the man began to crawl back up the stairs. Ethan saw the knife at the top—he'd dropped it before they fell. Ethan wanted to crawl up after him, but he couldn't get his arms and legs to work right.

Oh, shit. What if he'd broken his back in the fall? What if he was paralyzed?

No, he could still feel everything—and everything *hurt*—and with some effort he was able to get moving again, though not before the man had snatched up the knife and staggered down the hallway toward the woman's bedroom.

Move, asshole, he told himself. He ignored the pain and hurried back up the stairs.

The man went into the bedroom.

Ethan ran down the hallway after him.

The woman screamed.

Ethan could deal with the pain later. He ran into the bedroom, where the man stood next to the bed, the knife clenched tightly in his fist. The woman was trying to scramble away from him but she hadn't even made it to the other side of the bed.

The man raised the knife.

Ethan dove at him. Actually dove into the air, arms outstretched, and smashed into him.

The man's head struck the mattress. It was just a mattress, but he hit it *really* hard.

Ethan grabbed the back of his head by the hair and bashed him into the mattress over and over, as violently as he could, feeling a bit stupid but not having any other option at the moment.

He realized that the man had let go of the knife, so he yanked him up by the hair and shoved him to the side. The man struck the nightstand, knocking over a lamp, then fell to the floor.

Ethan picked up the knife.

The man's nose was bleeding badly and he looked stunned. Ethan kicked him in the chest, then crouched down next to him and pressed the blade to his throat.

"Move and I'll fucking kill you!" Ethan shouted.

The man spat out some blood. "Don't hurt me, please," he

said. "It's not my fault. They forced me to do this, okay? It's a game. They'll kill my family, okay?" He spat out some more blood. "I've got a wife. I've got three kids. I didn't want to do this."

Ethan didn't know what to say to that. Had he won? This counted as saving the woman, right?

"Where's my phone?" said the woman. "What happened to my phone? It was right here!"

"We're done, right?" Ethan asked the man.

The man nodded. "Just don't kill me."

Downstairs, the front door opened.

Ethan kept the knife to the man's throat as the stairs creaked. Sounded like more than one person.

Two men entered the bedroom, dressed entirely in black. They even had black facemasks. They were each holding a pistol.

"Move away from him," one of them told Ethan.

Ethan got up right away and moved to the other side of the room. The man wiped blood off his face and began to cry.

"I tried to get her," he said. "I almost did it! This isn't my fault!"

"That's not why we're here. You broke the rule."

"No! No, I didn't!"

"You told him you were in a game."

The man's eyes went wide with panic. "That didn't count! He was going to kill me! And he's part of the game too, right?" He looked over at Ethan. "You're part of it too, right?"

The men in facemasks pointed their pistols at him.

The old woman on the bed clapped her hands over her mouth in horror.

"You don't need to hurt him," said Ethan. "I won't say anything."

"Actually, we do," said one of the men. "If we don't punish him for breaking the rule, not only does he know we weren't serious, but you know we weren't serious. That's not good."

"*Please!*" the man wailed.

The men in facemasks opened fire. The man's body twitched as several silenced shots hit him in the face and chest. None of the bullets missed him. By the time he flopped over, they'd shot him at least ten times, which seemed to be more of a message to Ethan than necessary effort to kill the man.

The woman shrieked.

One of the men walked over to the bed. He pushed the woman back down onto her back, then picked up a pillow and pressed it against her face.

"You...you're not really going to kill her, are you?" Ethan asked.

The man who wasn't smothering the old woman nodded.

"But I saved her. I won."

"*You* won. You get the point. She loses. We obviously can't have her telling the caregiver what happened in the morning, right?"

Ethan's phone rang. "Please don't kill her," he said.

"She was dead as soon as we finalized the challenge. You can try to stop us, but I discourage it."

Ethan took his phone out of his pocket. It was Rick. He answered.

"Congratulations," said Rick. "I knew you could do it."

Ethan said nothing. The old woman struggled, but her kicks were already growing weaker.

"You're allowed to leave now," Rick said. "They'll take care of everything."

"I can't."

"You can't leave? Are you injured?"

Ethan couldn't explain it. There wasn't a damn thing he could do to save the woman's life, but walking out of the room while she was still being murdered seemed unspeakably cold hearted.

"No," he said. "I mean, I am injured, but I can walk. They're smothering the woman."

"Oh, I know. I'll call you back when you're on your way home."

Ethan wondered if the woman in the shallow grave would also have been eliminated, even if he'd dug her up in time. He saw no reason to ask. He was pretty sure he knew the answer.

The woman was barely struggling anymore.

She didn't even know Ethan was there. Why didn't he just leave the room? He sure as hell wasn't bringing her any peace in his final moments.

He waited.

The woman stopped moving. The man kept the pillow pressed against her face.

"We'll give it another minute or so," he said.

Ethan looked away from the woman, instead seeing the blood-soaked body of the other player. He looked down at the floor instead.

"All right, she's gone," said the man, removing the pillow. "I'm going to need you to leave us to our business now."

Ethan nodded and stood up.

"Hold up," said the man. "I didn't realize you'd been cut so bad. Let's get you patched up before you go."

"Thank you," said Ethan, barely able to believe the words came out of his mouth.

11

The man in the facemask applied a generous amount of antiseptic to the wound on Ethan's arm, and then taped gauze over it. "You'll need to keep changing the dressing," he said, giving Ethan a roll of additional gauze and some tape. "The cut isn't that deep but you sure don't want it to get infected."

"What do I tell my wife?" Ethan asked.

The man shrugged. "I dunno. That's your call. I'm just here to make sure you don't lose your arm."

RICK CALLED as Ethan drove home. "Congratulations again," he said. "I believed in you, even if you didn't believe in yourself."

"I never said I didn't believe in myself. When did self-doubt become part of this? It's like you're trying to say generic inspirational stuff without even thinking about the context."

"You're being antagonistic again."

"I watched a man get shot," said Ethan. "And I don't mean just shot in the chest, where his shirt could hide most of it, I mean I saw him take multiple bullet hits to the *face*. And then I watched an innocent old lady get smothered with a pillow. So yes, Rick, I'm feeling kind of rude right now."

"Nobody forced you to watch the old lady die."

"Eat my dick."

"Just remember who's on your side."

"Yeah, yeah, we're besties, I'm sorry, I forgot. So I guess I'm not the only player, huh?"

"Nope."

"Do I have to be worried that I'll be told to murder somebody?" Ethan asked.

"I'd worry about a lot of things."

"Great."

"But you earned a point tonight, so I hope you feel good about yourself."

"It's like you keep setting me up to be rude to you. How do you think I'm going to respond to that? Do you think I'm going to thank you for showing me how amazing I can be?"

"I'm trying to make the best of what I know isn't a high point in your life," said Rick.

"I met you in Vegas," said Ethan. "You followed me here to Kansas City. Where was the other guy from?"

"That's on a need-to-know basis, and you don't need to know."

"Did you make him travel here?"

"I'm not answering those kinds of questions about the game."

"I'd just like to know if I have to add sudden out of town trips to the list of things I have to lie to my wife about."

"It can't hurt to start thinking of cover stories."

"When does the game end? How many rounds are there?"

"Do you really think I'm going to tell you that?" asked Rick.

"Sure. Why not? If somebody's on *Survivor* they know that it's thirty-nine days. You know what it takes to win Monopoly."

"I guess that's a fair point," Rick admitted, "but I'm not authorized to tell you. All I can say is, go home and try to get a good night's sleep."

"Sure. No problem. It's not like I saw anything that'll give me a sleepless night."

EVERYBODY WAS in the living room when Ethan got home. Tim and Patrick were still playing the same video game, while Jenny sat on the couch reading a book, or at least pretending to read one.

"What happened to your arm?" she asked, quickly standing up.

The kids put the game on pause, a testament to how serious this seemed to be.

"It's no big deal," said Ethan. "I got cut at work."

"Did you put anything on it?"

"Yeah, it's fine. They took good care of me."

"Dad, you look kind of sick," said Patrick.

Ethan nodded. "I'm pretty tired."

"No, I mean sick. Like you're going to throw up."

"I'm not going to throw up, I promise. My job's a lot more stressful than it used to be, that's all."

"You should quit," said Tim.

"Then who would pay for your video games?"

"We'd just play the old ones."

"That's actually genuinely sweet," said Ethan. "But no, don't worry about me. I'm going to take a shower and go to bed."

"Don't you want dinner?" Jenny asked.

"Nah, I'm not hungry." If he tried to choke down some food, he probably *would* throw up.

"Okay."

Jenny looked really upset. And she was right to look that way. But did she look so upset that somebody watching might think she knew what was going on? Rick was already suspicious.

It would be okay. He'd been called out of the house with no notice and came home with a slashed arm. His wife would unquestionably look concerned in that scenario. It would be more suspicious if she had a cavalier attitude about it. He was just getting paranoid.

He took a long, scalding hot shower, scrubbing himself so thoroughly that it was painful. None of the executed man's blood had gotten on him, but Ethan scrubbed away as if he'd been drenched in it. The cut on his arm stung like hell under the hot water. At least it was only trickling blood instead of gushing it.

Jenny walked into the bathroom as he stepped out of the shower. She took a towel off the rack and handed to him.

"Actually, maybe one of the older ones from the back of the closet," Ethan said. "I don't want to get blood on the good ones."

Jenny retrieved one of their lesser towels. As he dried off, she got out the antiseptic and a box of bandages.

"So," she said. "How was work?"

"It sucked."

"Any idea when the overtime will stop?"

"No."

"Oh."

"I'm sorry."

"You don't have to be sorry. It's not your fault."

"It kind of is my fault."

"I need to know that we're all going to be okay when this is over," she said.

"We're going to be fine," said Ethan, and his eyes darted away from her for a split second, and he cursed himself for not being able to stop it from happening, because not being able to sustain eye contact was the classic "*I'm lying my ass off!*" signal. He might as well have covered his mouth.

Maybe she hadn't noticed.

She had totally noticed.

"Seriously, we're going to be fine," he said, stumbling over the words. He desperately needed to convey the message of "*We have to keep up this ruse, because less than an hour ago I watched a guy get shot to death for violating the rule,*" but he had no idea how to do it without breaking the rule.

Jenny said nothing. She absolutely did not believe that they were going to be fine.

And if she didn't believe that, what would stop her from fleeing with their children?

What would stop her from calling the police?

"I promise you it's all good," he said. "I'll keep working, and I'll get our head above water and then I'll quit. At least I know that I'll never gamble again. I'll probably have to go into therapy if I ever see a slot machine. So, yes, right now my unpredictable schedule sucks, but you have nothing to worry about. I'm going to take care of you. I'm going to take care of the kids. Our family is fine."

"If you say so," said Jenny. "Let's get your arm bandaged up."

She applied the antiseptic with a cotton ball and as he winced in pain Ethan searched her face for signs as to what she might be thinking. There was no way for her not to be scared, but he needed her not to be so scared that she decided it was worth it to break the rules. But he couldn't convey that without breaking the rules.

He tried to think of a way to share that message in coded language, making it clear what he meant without tipping off any eavesdroppers, but he immediately rejected every phrasing as too transparent. His mind wasn't working in top-notch condition at the moment.

It was too risky.

He'd have to trust that she wouldn't do something dangerous.

After she bandaged him up, he put on boxer briefs and a t-shirt (he hoped Rick had been suffering through a nice unobstructed view of his dick) and got into bed. Jenny kissed him on the forehead.

"Do you promise everything will be fine?"

Don't look away. Don't look away. Don't look away. Don't blink.

"I promise," he said.

"All right. I'll come to bed soon."

Jenny left the bedroom. Ethan fell asleep seconds later.

He woke up to the sound of his phone ringing.

What time was it? The clock on the nightstand said 12:00. No way.

He picked up the phone and, yes, it was Rick calling. The same night? Was he serious?

It might have been okay for him to let this call go to voice mail and pick up on the second call, when he'd left the bedroom and could speak more privately, but after tonight's double murder he was much more frightened of defying Rick.

"Hello?" he asked.

"Hi, Ethan. Did I wake you up?"

Ethan slid his legs over the side of the bed. "I hope you're joking. I just got back from work."

"Oh, I'm so sorry. Did you think you'd get some time for R&R before your next challenge? Did I say anything to imply that?"

"Yes, actually. You told me to get a good night's sleep."

"You're right. I did. I hope you got part of a good night's sleep. Tell your wife you have to go back to work and get in your car. I'll call you back in five minutes."

Rick hung up. Ethan literally wanted to just start crying. This was unreal.

Jenny, of course, was awake.

"I have to go," he said.

She sat up, scooted over, and took his hand. "We'll get through this," she told him. "Like you said, the weird work hours will go away after we make up the shortfall."

"Yeah. Try to go back to sleep."

Ethan quickly got dressed and went out to the car. He didn't even want to look in the rearview mirror, because he probably looked like somebody you'd cross the street to avoid. *Don't hurt me, sir. Here's some money.*

Rick called.

"Are you outside of your house?" Rick asked.

"You don't know?"

"I do know. I was seeing if you'd be honest."

"Yeah, I'm in my car."

"Are you ready for your next challenge?"

"No."

"Are you saying that you're not ready, or that you're declining it?"

"I'll hear what you have to say, but why should I bother accepting? I accepted the last challenge because I didn't want a woman to get stabbed to death. I saved her and she died anyway. So it was all a great big waste."

"You earned a point," said Rick.

"So I earned a point. So what? I didn't drive out there to earn a point in your game, I drove out there to stop a woman from being murdered by some whack-nut with a knife. Now I know that there's no purpose to playing. I might as well not even bother."

"That's not a winning attitude."

"What's the challenge?"

"This time you have a 25% chance of succeeding."

"Oh, for fuck's sake."

"It would be boring if the game got easier."

"And I'm playing for a point?" Ethan asked.

"No. You're playing for a briefcase filled with ten pounds of cocaine."

"I don't want ten pounds of cocaine."

"I'm sure you don't," said Rick. "But the drug dealers who believe you have their shipment would very much like it back."

Ethan didn't even know what to say to this. He just sat in his car, staring through the front windshield, unable to believe that this was his life now.

"Ethan...?"

"I thought coke was measured in kilos."

"So you'll win about four and a half kilos of coke that was supposed to be delivered to some extremely vengeful criminals. You could return it to them, no questions asked."

"You know what? No."

"No?"

"I'm calling bullshit. I don't buy it. Maybe you can set up some game where one player tries to kill an old lady and the other player tries to save her, but you expect me to believe that you stole a briefcase of cocaine from drug dealers and have framed me for it?"

"*Will* frame you for it."

"I don't believe you."

"That's interesting. I didn't expect this."

"So yes, I'm declining. I'm going back to bed."

"I'd be lying if I said I wasn't completely shocked," said Rick. "I hope you have a restful night of sleep, and I hope this works out for you."

"G'night." Ethan hung up.

It had to be bullshit.

Right?

Ethan was suddenly having very serious doubts. Why *wouldn't* these psychopaths add vengeful gangsters to the mix? It was the next logical step to this insanity! What the hell was he thinking?

He called Rick back.

"Yes?" Rick answered. "May I help you?"

"Can I take it back?"

"Hmmm. I'm not quite sure. Let me consult my rulebook."

"Seriously, Rick, let me take it back. I wasn't thinking right. I'm exhausted. I'm stressed out. I apologize."

"What are you apologizing for? Skipping this round, or for the verbal abuse?"

"Anything. Everything." Ethan hated how frantic he sounded. "I'll apologize for whatever you want."

"An all-encompassing apology like that probably isn't sincere," said Rick. "I don't want your apology. Now, the good news is that I'm empowered to let you take back your terrible decision. The bad news is that I'm not empowered to do so without you incurring a penalty. There was a time element to this challenge, so I'm reducing your time by fifteen minutes, which I'd say knocks you down to a 20% of success."

"All right. I'll take it. What's the challenge?"

"I'll call you back in fifteen minutes. Stay in your car and try not to go completely mad before then."

12

Ethan felt like he'd already gone mad. He passed the time by watching cute otter videos on his phone.

Finally, exactly fifteen minutes later, Rick called him back.

"You didn't change your mind again, did you?" Rick asked.

"No."

"Glad to hear it. So, Ethan, you get to go on a scavenger hunt! Race from clue to clue, and waiting at the end is some pure and uncut product. Hell, you can keep it for yourself if you want, or skim a little off the top. No judgment here."

"Did you get a bit slaphappy while we were waiting?" Ethan asked.

"A bit, yeah. First clue. It's an easy one. Look where you saved the kids. Got it?"

"Got it."

"On your mark...get set...*go*!"

Rick hung up. Ethan started the car and almost knocked over

his mailbox as he backed out of the driveway. Then he sped off toward the playground.

When he arrived there, he parked the car and realized that he didn't have a flashlight. He popped open the trunk and checked, but this time nobody had been considerate enough to leave one there. The streetlamp would have to do.

He ran to the sandbox. As he stepped inside, he wondered if there were more hypodermic needles buried in there. Frantically digging through the sand in dim light with unprotected hands could end very badly.

Ethan hurried back to the car. He should've thought of this before going to the sandbox. He didn't know how much time he had, but he knew he couldn't waste any.

He didn't have any gloves in the car. He did have an old grease-covered towel, which would have to be good enough. He wrapped it around his hand as he ran back to the sandbox, and then began to dig.

He didn't even know what he was looking for. A tiny piece of paper? A box? He'd just have to dig and look for anything that wasn't sand.

After about half a minute, he found something.

A hypodermic needle.

He'd love to slam this into Rick's smug face.

Ethan continued digging. Found another one. Then another.

How many goddamn hypodermic needles were buried in this sandbox?

He kept going, hoping the towel was enough to protect him from getting jabbed with whatever shit was in these things.

Found another one.

Wait. He should learn from his mistakes. Maybe the clue was

written on the needle. He held it up, trying to search for writing somewhere on the surface.

He couldn't see well enough to tell.

He gathered all of the needles and carried them closer to the streetlight, then inspected each of them.

No writing.

He went back to the sandbox and continued searching, finding two more needles within a matter of seconds. He'd gather a couple more before running back to the light.

His hands were shaking.

Was he missing something? Were the needles a clue that he simply wasn't getting?

He kept digging.

Another needle. And another. And another.

And then something green. A small envelope.

He tore it open and unfolded the paper inside.

Look where you failed to save the woman.

Technically, he'd failed to save two women, but this presumably was referring to the woman who'd been buried alive. He hoped the clues continued to be this straightforward.

Though he hated to leave a sandbox full of hypodermic needles, it was after midnight and he couldn't imagine that any little kids would show up for playtime after dark. When this was over, he'd return to the playground and put up signs to warn people not to go into the sandbox.

He took the needles with him and returned to his car.

He almost put them in the glove compartment, but he didn't know what was in them. He had a vision of getting pulled over by a cop and having a dozen hypodermic needles fall out of the glove compartment when he went to get his registration.

Instead, he put them in the trunk and covered them with the towel.

Not having a flashlight would be much more of a problem if he was trying to find the location of the grave in Rendill Park. He hated to lose the time, but he had to return home.

He'd had no reason to think he needed extra equipment—the last time it had been thoughtfully provided for him.

Was he allowed to call Jenny to have her meet him outside with a flashlight?

Sure, why not? He wasn't allowed to tell her about the game, but this would be part of the lie.

He texted her instead of calling. Less chance of one of them accidentally giving something away. He assumed they were monitoring his text messages, though it was possible that the idea that they *might* be reading his texts was supposed to be enough to keep him on the honor system.

There might be digging involved, but they didn't own a shovel. A flashlight could be innocuous, but he didn't want Jenny to wonder why he needed a shovel after midnight.

When he pulled into their driveway, Jenny was there with a flashlight. He rolled down the window and she handed it to him without a word. Then he sped off to Rendill Park.

It was the same deal as before. The gate kept him from driving into the actual park, so he left the car behind. He walked a hundred paces forward, then fifty paces to the left. It was easy to find the place he'd dug before, though he was disappointed that there wasn't a green envelope resting on top of the freshly overturned dirt.

He knelt down and began to dig with his hands.

The ground was soft and it went quickly. He was careful to

make sure he didn't toss aside any clumps of dirt big enough to conceal an envelope.

About two feet down, the same distance as before, his fingers scraped against cardboard.

He scooped away more dirt. It was the same type of box as before.

He got enough dirt out of the way that he could open the lid.

Ethan gasped and recoiled. Another woman was inside. She was bound and gagged, her eyes wide with terror.

He lifted her up. The gag was difficult to untie, and he didn't have anything to cut it with, but he finally got it off. She leaned forward and violently coughed for a few moments while he untied her hands and feet.

He helped her out of the grave, which was difficult because she could barely move. He tried to get her to her feet, but she turned into dead weight and he almost dropped her.

"Are your legs numb?" he asked.

She nodded. "It's all numb."

"Do you want me to carry you?"

She nodded again, then she began to cry.

Ethan shined the flashlight beam around the inside of the thick cardboard box to make sure there wasn't an envelope in there. He saw nothing. He assumed that the woman either knew the clue or had it on her.

He hoisted her into his arms and carried her to the paved road. She wasn't as emaciated as the first woman who'd been buried alive, but she still didn't look like she had three hot meals a day very often.

Now she was sobbing.

He set her down. He didn't want to leave the park until he knew she had the clue.

She'd had a deeply traumatic experience, so he could give her a few minutes to compose herself. He'd be sobbing, too.

A few minutes later, she hadn't stopped. He gently helped her to her feet.

Ethan didn't want to make this awkward, but he did kind of need the clue. He didn't know how many more parts there were to this scavenger hunt or how long he had to complete them.

He wasn't good at consoling people. He tried to give her a comforting hug, but she flinched and pulled away.

"I'm sorry," he said.

She said something back that he couldn't understand.

"Do you know who did this to you?" he asked.

She shook her head.

"Do you know anything about a clue?"

"What clue?"

"I'm looking for a clue."

"What clue?"

She had to have the clue, right? The "don't tell anybody about the game" couldn't apply to a woman who he'd just dug up in order to obtain a clue. "I'm on a scavenger hunt," he said.

The woman gave him a blank stare.

"What's your name?" Ethan asked.

"Tammy."

"Hi, Tammy. I'm Ethan. I wish we could've met under different circumstances. I'm on a scavenger hunt. The reason I found you is because my next clue was in that spot. So I need to know if you have the clue."

She dropped back onto the pavement and began to sob again. Then she started tearing at her hair.

What was he supposed to do? In any other situation, the interrogation could wait, but he desperately needed the clue.

Ethan sat down next to her. "I'll get you to a hospital," he said. "I'll get you some help. I just need to know if anybody said anything to you about a clue."

"What clue?"

"Any clue."

The next obvious location was the house where the old lady had been murdered, but that was pretty far to travel without knowing for sure, and he didn't want to have to search an entire two-story home. The clue had to be here. Maybe he needed to pull the cardboard coffin entirely out of the ground and check the entire thing.

"Is there anything in your pocket?" he asked.

She shoved her hands into each pocket. "No."

"Nothing in your...bra or anything?"

"Address?" Tammy asked.

"What?"

"Address?"

"Do you have an address for me?"

Tammy just stared at him.

"What do you mean by address?" Ethan asked.

"I got an address. I think." She wiped her eyes with the back of her hand. "I'm sorry."

"No, no, don't apologize. You're doing fine. You've been through a lot. Are you saying that somebody gave you an address?"

"Yeah," she said. "Yeah, I think. Yeah, yeah. He did. An address."

"Do you remember it?"

Tammy closed her eyes.

"Do you remember the address?"

"I'm *thinking!*" she screamed.

"All right, that's fine, take your time."

"One," Tammy said. "One two? One three? One something."

"One something. That's a start."

"One two one. One two one one? No. One two one. I think."

"One twenty-one. That's good."

"One two one, not one twenty-one."

"One two one. Do you remember the street?"

Tammy shook her head.

"It's really important that you remember the street," said Ethan. "Do you remember the first letter?"

"No."

"Just try to think. Relax. We've got all the time in the world."

"Maybe an H."

"An H. Excellent. We're making a lot of progress."

"Or an R."

"Okay, those are two very different letters, but that's fine, we've still narrowed it down."

"I can't remember," said Tammy. "I just can't remember."

"But they told you something, right?"

"I guess."

"It'll come to you. You're really stressed out right now. Do you want to take some deep breaths with me?"

"No, I don't want to take any fucking deep breaths! I want to go home!"

"I'll take you home," said Ethan. "Where's home?"

"My arm hurts."

He looked at her arm. She was bleeding through her long-sleeve shirt.

"Let me take a look," said Ethan.

"Don't touch my arm."

"Let's see how bad it is."

"It's bad."

"Did you cut yourself when I pulled you out of there?"

"I think they did it."

"The people who buried you alive cut your arm?"

Tammy nodded.

"Can I see?"

"No."

"Please?"

Tammy pulled up her sleeve. Letters had been carved into her arm.

121 Roberts Lane.

"Oh," she said.

"I need you to come with me," Ethan told her. "I don't think you're safe." Nobody had said he had to leave Tammy behind, and if he didn't bring her along, he assumed she'd meet a similar fate to the old woman.

"None of us are safe."

"No, but you'll be safer with me." He didn't even know if that was true. "Let's go. We need to move fast."

He took Tammy by the hand and they hurried out of the park. She stood in front of his car as if she'd never seen a motor vehicle before, but when he opened the door for her she got inside.

He put "*121 Roberts Lane*" into his GPS. Fourteen minutes away. Not bad.

As they drove away, Tammy leaned against the door and just stared out the front windshield, looking comatose. Ethan was too busy with his own thoughts to try to make conversation, so they drove in silence.

He made it to the house in eleven minutes.

This was most definitely not the kind of place he'd normally visit, even in the daytime, even with a couple of friends. There were several cars in the driveway and loud music coming from inside. Ethan had never personally been to a crack house, and perhaps he was wrong because he was the furthest thing from an expert in such matters, but this place had an extremely strong "crack house" vibe.

Or maybe it was a meth den. Either way, no sane person would knock on that door in the middle of the night.

Ethan did not have the option of being sane.

13

"Stay in the car," he told Tammy.

"Can you leave the keys so I can listen to music?" she asked.

"Sorry, no," he said. He didn't want to be a jerk, but he also didn't want to come back out and discover that she'd stolen his car. He wasn't thinking, "There's no way this night could get any worse!" There were plenty of ways this night could get worse, and having his car get stolen would be a big one.

"What if they come after me?"

"If you speed off in my car, then *I'm* screwed. You can come with me if you want, but I don't know what's going to happen in there."

"I'll wait," Tammy said.

Ethan got out of the car. The last thing he wanted to do was go up and knock on that door. In fact, he considered that this might be more dangerous than having drug dealers think he had a suitcase of their goods.

But right now it was just him in danger. If he failed, Jenny and the kids might be in danger. Or not. There was a lot of unexplained stuff in the rules of this game. Either way, he thought his best course of action was to try to successfully complete his 20% chance of finishing this round of the game.

He walked up to the front door.

He could not believe he was going to do this.

He knocked on the door.

Waited.

Nobody answered. Maybe they couldn't hear him above the music.

He knocked again, louder.

The door swung open. A young skinny guy with hair that stuck up on the left side answered. He blinked a few times as if unused to the light, even though it was dark outside. "Yeah?"

"Hi," Ethan said. "This is going to sound weird—"

"You a cop?"

"No."

"Prove it. Say 'I'm not a cop.'"

"I'm not a cop."

"You look too scared to be a cop anyway. You buyin'?"

"No. I'm looking for a clue."

The skinny guy laughed. "You're in the wrong place, dude. I don't know anybody who's got a clue about anything."

"I was told to come here to get a clue. You may not be the right person to talk to."

"Do you mean get a clue as in expand your mind? I could get you some shrooms, maybe. Not sure if I have some or not. I could look."

"No, I'm not here to buy any drugs."

"Shrooms aren't drugs. They're all natural. God makes them."

"I just want the clue. Is there anybody else in there I can talk to?"

"Yeah, it's party time in here. C'mon in."

Ethan followed him into the house. There were at least a dozen people inside, and a thin but pungent cloud of smoke. Beer cans were everywhere. The kitchenette counter was piled high with garbage and dirty dishes. One wall was lined with multiple plastic tubs of kitty litter that didn't look like they'd been scooped out in weeks.

There was absolutely nothing about this house to dissuade him of the notion that it was a crack house.

"Hey!" the skinny guy shouted. "Hey! Hey!" When nobody heard him, he walked over to the stereo and turned off the music, eliciting several angry reactions. He pointed to Ethan. "This dude is looking for a clue!"

"You a private eye?" asked a man who sat on the armrest of a couch.

"No. And I'm not a cop. I'm on a scavenger hunt, and I was given this address for my next clue."

"Scavenger hunt? That sounds fun as shit. Can I play?"

"Does anybody know what I'm talking about?" Ethan asked. His heart was racing and he was having a little bit of trouble catching his breath, but he tried not to show how scared he was.

Everybody looked around at each other and shook their heads.

"Nobody knows? Somebody here is supposed to have a clue for me."

"Nah, dude, nobody has your clue," said the skinny guy. He pulled over a chair. "But have a seat. Party with us."

"I really shouldn't."

"Have a seat. Party with us." He wasn't *quite* threatening, but nor was he suggesting that this was completely optional.

Ethan sat down.

"You sure you don't want anything?" the skinny guy asked. "You sure don't need any uppers, but you're definitely a dude who could use some weed."

"No, thank you. I appreciate it, though."

A woman plopped right onto his lap. Her hair was unwashed and stringy, and if she'd had any breasts to speak of, they would've popped out of the tiny top she wore. "Hey, sexy."

The skinny guy laughed. "Don't go getting any ideas. She's not free."

"I'm free," she said. "Just not *free*, if you know what I mean."

"He knew what I meant."

"I didn't even know what you meant."

"I'm really not in the market for that," said Ethan. "I swear, I'm just here for the clue."

"You sure?" the skinny guy asked. "I'd tap that ass. She's pretty much clean."

She took a swing at him. "Shut up, dickhead."

"I'm kidding, I'm kidding. I mean, you'd wear a rubber, obviously, and you'd run out and get a shot of penicillin as soon as you can, but other than that, she's clean. We'll give you a good rate. We'll pretend you have a Groupon."

Everybody around them laughed.

Ethan tried to stand up, but the girl wouldn't get off his lap.

"Again, I'm not here for anything like that. I guess I have the wrong address."

"Naw, dude, you've got the right address. Look at her! She'll do anything you tell her to!"

"Not *anything*," she protested.

"Anything that don't leave marks."

"That's true."

"You might catch some of the smaller diseases, but it won't be anything that kills you. She's worth getting a shot for. Trust me."

The girl licked the side of Ethan's face. He immediately got up, almost causing her to fall onto the floor. "I have to go."

A bearded guy sitting on the couch sniffed something off the back of his hand. "You like games, huh?"

"I used to. Not anymore."

"You like Russian Roulette?"

"No."

He held up a revolver. "I'll play you some Russian Roulette right now."

"That won't be necessary."

"Who's in for some Russian Roulette?" he asked everybody in the room.

Nobody indicated that they were, though several of them laughed.

"I'm trying not to die tonight," said Ethan.

"That's fair." The bearded guy pressed his palm against the barrel of the gun. "What about hands? We see who gets a hole shot in his hand first?"

"You can shoot off your hand if you want," said the skinny guy, "but I ain't taking you to the hospital, and you're cleaning the blood off my couch."

"This little gun couldn't shoot my hand off. It would go all the way through, yeah, but I'd still have a hand attached to my wrist."

"I don't want to see anybody's hand come off," said the woman who'd been sitting on Ethan's lap.

Ethan needed to get the hell out of here. He didn't even want the clue anymore. He couldn't imagine that they would've taken the time to carve an address onto Tammy's arm and get it wrong, but this was going nowhere.

"I'm sorry to have disturbed you," he said, taking a step toward the door.

"No, don't go," said the skinny guy. "I'm intrigued. You're an intriguing guy. Am I using that word right? Intriguing. I think I'm right. I didn't even know how to pronounce it until a couple of years ago. I thought it was *in-tree-gyoo-ing*. What a dumbass, huh? You need to party with us. You don't have to go all wild and stuff. Let's have some fun."

"Russian Roulette!" said the bearded man.

"Put the damn gun away."

"Who's gonna make me? I've got a gun."

Ethan tried to move closer to the door, but the skinny guy stepped in his way. Ethan was confident that one punch would solve this problem, yet while he was sure he could kick this guy's ass, he could not kick the asses of everybody in the house, especially when at least one of them had a gun.

Should he lay him out and run?

He wasn't sure he could make it to the car before the others got him.

And if the address *was* correct after all, this would make it a lot more difficult to get the clue out of them. He just needed to leave the house, call Rick, and beg for some kind of guidance.

"I need to go out and make a call," said Ethan.

"Make the call here. None of us will listen."

"Let me leave, okay?"

"Don't you like us? Don't you think we're friendly? I offered you the chance to tap some ass. That's pretty friendly. You would have had an enjoyable time. I don't even know you, and here I am trying to make sure you have a pleasant night, and yet you're being anti-social. I don't appreciate it."

It was obvious that Ethan needed to try a different approach. He needed to pretend to have infinitely more courage than he was actually feeling right now. He had to assume that these people were just messing with him, that they didn't actually intend to keep him here against his will, so if he got stern with them they might let him through.

"Look, asshole," he said, immediately wondering if "asshole" was taking it too far. "I'm here for the clue, and nothing else. If you don't have it, then there's no reason for me to stick around, so I'd like you to get the hell out of my way so I can keep searching." He could see on the skinny guy's face that "asshole" had definitely been too far, but it was too late now. If he apologized, he'd never get to leave.

The skinny guy stepped out of his way. "You were bringing the party down anyway. And you don't smell good."

"What the shit is going on in here?" a booming voice asked.

Ethan turned around. A man had emerged from a back room. A very large man in his thirties, well over six feet tall, wearing a white t-shirt with several brown stains on the front. He hadn't shaved in a while. He had a unibrow, except there was a missing strip just over the edge of his left eye, making it look like he had one really long eyebrow and one really short one. He had quite a belly on him, but his arms were thick.

"Yo, Grendie, this guy is looking for a scavenger hunt clue," said the skinny guy.

"Then why didn't somebody wake me up?"

"You didn't tell us to wake you up."

"The shit I didn't! I told Benny to wake me up if somebody came here looking for a clue."

Some guy, presumably Benny, snapped out of a trance. "Huh? What?"

Grendie walked across the room. The floor didn't shake with each step, but Ethan could imagine that it did, accompanied by a musical theme. Nobody in the house seemed happy that Grendie was awake. The skinny guy stepped far out of the way.

Ethan was hugely relieved to have finally found somebody who knew what he was talking about, though the sight of Grendie walking right toward him was not one that gave him peace of mind. Ethan couldn't quite identify the aroma that wafted from him, but anything that could compete with the other foul smells in this place deserved respect.

"You looking for a clue?"

"Yes, sir," said Ethan.

"I'll sell it to you."

"How much?"

"No, I take that back. I'll fight you for it."

"I'm not here to fight anybody."

"Well, fucking duh. I know you didn't come here to fight me. But you're here, and I'm here, and when I get woke up out of a sound sleep, I like to fight."

"I'll happily buy it from you," said Ethan.

"Are you deaf? I said I wanted to fight. You want the clue bad enough, you'll fight me for it."

"I can't beat you in a fight," said Ethan. "I mean that as a compliment."

"Not in a one-on-one fistfight, no," said Grendie. "We'll figure out a way to make it more fair."

"Fire!" somebody shouted. "Fight each other with lighters and aerosol cans!"

"Do we have any aerosol cans?" Grendie asked.

"I'll run out and get some right now if you do it."

"Naw," said the skinny guy. "We can't be shooting streams of fire indoors."

"Well, you could take it outdoors, I guess. That would still be fun to watch."

"Knives," said Grendie.

"No," said Ethan. "I'm not going to have a knife fight with you."

"Do you want the clue or not?"

"Not bad enough for a knife fight."

"Oh, I think you do," said Grendie. "I'm not saying we'll fight to the death. I get why you'd say no to that. What we'll do is, the first person to get three cuts on his opponent wins. You win, I give you the clue. I win, you walk out of here with no clue and three cuts. Sound fair?"

Everybody but Ethan reacted with great joy to this idea.

"I'll get the knives," said the skinny guy, hurrying over to the kitchen area.

"This party sounded like everybody was having a lot of fun," said Ethan. "Why mess up the vibe?"

"Oh, there's no party that can't be improved with a knife

fight!" Grendie smiled, revealing teeth that were unsurprisingly discolored and low in number.

This had to be a joke, right? They weren't really going to make him participate in a knife fight. Was this an official element of the game, part of the reason he only had a 20% chance to succeed, or was Grendie making up his own rules? Ethan supposed it didn't matter. Unless Grendie burst out into laughter and said, "Juuuuuuuust kidding," it appeared that Ethan was going to have his very first knife fight.

The skinny guy returned. He had a butcher knife in one hand and a meat cleaver in the other.

"What the shit is that?" asked Grendie, pointing to the meat cleaver.

The skinny guy looked confused. "You don't know what a meat cleaver is?"

"I know what one is. It's not a knife."

"It's *like* a knife. I didn't think it would be fair if one of you had a great big butcher knife and the other one had some dull butter knife."

"Why do you even have a meat cleaver? What kind of meat are you cleaving? When was the last time you prepared an actual meal in this place?"

"It was my grandma's meat cleaver."

Grendie reached for one of the weapons, but the skinny guy stepped back. "Uh-uh, wait, hold on now. You don't get to just grab the one you want. It's gotta be fair. Heads or tails?"

"Heads," said Grendie.

"I don't have a coin, but I was thinking tails." He looked at Ethan. "Which do you want?"

"I want his grandmother's meat cleaver."

"Aw, that's a low class move," said Grendie, but he didn't stop the skinny guy from handing Ethan the meat cleaver. Ethan gave it a test swing. He really, really, really did not want to do this.

Grendie took the butcher knife and gave it a test swing as well.

"The rules," said Grendie. "Slash but don't stab. Don't jab your blade into anybody's eye. Cuts don't count unless they draw blood. You can quit like a scared little bitch whenever you want, but then you don't get the clue. Are you clear?"

"I'm clear," said Ethan.

"All right, then. On the count of three. One...two..."

"Whoa, whoa," said the skinny guy. "You don't get to count down your own fight. I'll do it."

"Fine."

"You were also counting in the wrong direction. Should be three, two, one, not one, two, three. I think. Maybe I'm wrong. Your way might have been right. Shit."

"Just count," said Grendie.

"One...two...three!"

Grendie let out what sounded like a werewolf howl, then lunged forward with the butcher knife.

14

T*ampa, Florida. Two minutes earlier.*

"I'm only going to ask you one more time," said the man in the dark suit. "Where's my briefcase?"

"I don't have it," Harry French insisted. "I've never had it. I swear to God, this is all a mistake!"

The man scowled. "Are you saying I'm prone to errors? Are you saying I've been given faulty intelligence?"

"I'm not saying anything except that I don't have your drugs!"

"Drugs? I never said anything about drugs. How do you know the briefcase wasn't full of collectibles?" He nodded to the bulky man who stood at his side. "Hit him again."

The bulky man punched Harry in the stomach. He almost fell over this time, but braced himself against his big-screen television.

"I know it was you," said the man in the dark suit. "I have pictures of you taking it from the drop spot."

"They're fake!"

"Oh, they're fake? I've been staring at Photoshopped pictures all this time? Gosh, well, I'm so sorry for this wacky misunderstanding. I guess we'll be on our way, then."

The bulky man punched Harry again. This time he did fall.

"I got these pictures from a trusted source. I trust him a hell of a lot more than I trust you. Now, if you're saying that you can't get my briefcase back, then I might as well just kill you right now."

"Please—"

"Please kill you? Put you out of your misery?" He reached into the inside pocket of his suit and took out a pistol. "Don't be too impatient. I've got to get the silencer on here first. We don't want to disturb your neighbors, right?"

Harry tried to get back to his feet, but lost his balance and fell again.

The man began to screw the silencer onto the barrel of his revolver. "I could've had this on the gun already, but I'm doing it now so you know that shit is about to get real. By which I mean, you have one more chance to tell me where my briefcase is."

"I can get it."

"I don't believe you. You were more credible when you said you didn't know what I was talking about. You swear you can get it?"

"Yes!"

"You're not just trying to stall for time?"

"No!"

"All right. I'm still going to shoot you—I'm just not going to kill you or incapacitate you. Four flesh wounds. One across each leg, and one across each arm. You'll bleed but I'll take you to a guy who can patch you up. He's not licensed but he's good. You ready?"

"Please don't shoot me," said Harry.

"You're getting a pretty sweet deal. I wouldn't complain if I were you. We'll do the left leg first." The man crouched down and placed the barrel of the pistol against Harry's upper leg. "It's going to go in here..." He tapped the other side of Harry's leg with his index finger. "...and come out there. Which sounds really bad, and kind of is, but it won't go deep. It'll stay near the surface. It'll hit the bookcase when it comes out. I don't want to mess up your books, so how about you turn around—like this—yeah, like that—see, now it'll hit the wall. All set? Say yes or I'll shoot you in the head."

"Yes," said Harry.

The man squeezed the trigger. Harry screamed.

"I apologize," said the man. "I got the angle wrong on that. It's okay. We've got three more chances to get it right."

GRENDIE's first swing with the butcher knife missed, but not by much.

His second swing, which he was able to get in before Ethan did his first, slashed Ethan across the left arm, crisscrossing the cut that was already there and slicing right through the bandage.

Ethan winced in pain.

"First cut already!" said Grendie, holding up his arms in victory. "It's like you don't even want the clue."

"Hold up, does that count as one or two?" asked the skinny guy. "He's bleeding on both sides of the bandage. I think he needs to take it off so we can see if it's one continuous cut or if the bandage blocked part of it."

"What the shit kind of loopholes are you trying to find?" asked Grendie. "It's one cut."

"Just trying to help you out."

"You think I need your help? I don't need to win this on a technicality. Go somewhere else. Nobody appointed you referee."

The skinny guy hung his head and stepped out of the way.

"You ready?" Grendie asked Ethan.

"Yeah."

They both lunged at each other at the same time. Both missed.

"Nice one," said Grendie. "I felt the air swish."

Grendie slashed at him again. This swing would have, if it hit its mark, cut Ethan from nipple to nipple. He stepped back out of the way and tripped on one of the hundreds of pieces of garbage on the floor. He reached out to keep his balance, grabbing the woman who'd been on his lap. They both struck the floor.

Grendie laughed. "I'll let you get up."

Ethan got up. Something was stuck to the back of his shirt but he didn't reach back there to find out what it was.

"No more freebies," Grendie told him. "We're playing for real now."

"He grabbed my tit," said the woman. "That's ten bucks."

"He grabbed your arm," said Grendie. "I saw it."

"Then you weren't watching very close."

Grendie lunged at Ethan with the butcher knife. Missed again. There was no rule saying that Ethan had to stay in the same general area, so he hurried past a few people into the kitchen area.

Grendie followed.

Ethan quickly spun around, hoping that Grendie's momentum would take him right into the blade.

It didn't.

Grendie swung the knife. The blade slashed across Ethan's knuckles and he dropped the meat cleaver.

Ethan looked at his hand. It wasn't bleeding. "It didn't break the skin."

"You need to sharpen this thing," Grendie called out to the skinny guy. Then he swung the knife again before Ethan could even think about retrieving his weapon.

Ethan grabbed a frying pan off the counter, which stuck to a plate, which stuck to a fork. He took a swing at Grendie's head that fell short, though the fork came loose and almost hit a woman who was standing in the corner.

"He can't use other weapons!" said the skinny guy.

"That wasn't in the rules!" said Ethan. He might only get credit for cutting Grendie with the meat cleaver, but that didn't mean he couldn't knock him unconscious with a frying pan first.

He took another swing. This time the plate came loose and struck Grendie's face. It fell to the floor and shattered.

Grendie had previously seemed to be having fun with this whole experience. Based on his expression, that was no longer the case.

He stabbed at Ethan with the butcher knife. Ethan deflected it by using the frying pan as a shield. Grendie lunged with the knife, aiming lower this time, and the tip of the blade tore across Ethan's side. He cried out and clutched the wound.

"Let's see it," said Grendie.

Ethan removed his hand and held up his bloody palm.

"Two to zero," said Grendie.

Ethan bolted away. He scrambled back around the counter and picked up the meat cleaver. He almost felt like he should just hold out his arm, accept the third and final cut, and hope they'd finally let him leave. But no, he'd keep trying, even if he was quite clearly not going to win this.

Grendie came around the corner, swishing the butcher knife back and forth, trying very successfully to be intimidating.

Ethan backed away.

Then he lost his balance. Somebody had tripped him intentionally. He wanted to protest, but if he could use a frying pan, he had to accept that there was no specific rule about a spectator purposely tripping him.

Ethan landed on something spongy.

He deeply regretted making Grendie so angry. The huge man lumbered toward him, then dropped to his knees, hovering right over him. He wasn't going to try to kill him, was he? He certainly had a homicidal look on his face.

He slammed the knife down.

Ethan slashed with the meat cleaver.

Grendie's eyes went wide.

His hand went to his throat.

Ethan had not intended to slash at his neck. It had just been a blind slash, trying to defend himself.

How deep had he cut Grendie?

Blood trickled through Grendie's fingers and rained down upon Ethan's chest.

Pretty deep.

Ethan scooted out of the way.

Everybody stared silently as blood continued to spew out between Grendie's fingers. He dropped the butcher knife. Then he flopped forward.

None of the people in the house moved.

Ethan got up. "It was an accident," he insisted. "You saw what he was trying to do. He would have killed me."

Nobody said anything.

"I'm leaving," said Ethan, cautiously making his way toward the door.

He'd killed somebody. Slashed a man's throat with a meat cleaver. Accident or not, he'd taken a human life.

He needed to save his complete mental breakdown for later. For now, he just needed to get out of this house.

Everybody just watched him as he continued moving toward the door.

"No," the skinny guy finally said. "You murdered our friend. You ain't going anywhere."

Ethan frantically shook his head. "It wasn't a murder."

"Everybody saw it."

"Good! So everybody saw that I was defending myself!"

"I saw you open up his neck!"

"He was out of control. Somebody call 911."

Nobody took out their cell phones. It was immediately clear that none of them wanted the police to show up here, even if it was to save their friend.

Grendie was beyond saving, anyway. The pool of blood was expanding rapidly. A plastic wrapper was floating away in it.

Ethan took another step toward the door.

"You stay where you are," the skinny guy said.

Ethan swung the meat cleaver back and forth in the air. A droplet of blood struck the woman who'd been on his lap.

"We have to kill him, right?" the skinny guy asked the others. "We can't let him walk on out of here."

The woman wiped the speck of blood off her face. "Yeah, let's kill him."

RICK, Gavin, and Butch sat in the back of the van, listening to the audio feed they were drawing from Ethan's phone.

"I'm going to try to get permission to pull him out of there," said Rick.

"They won't go for it," said Gavin. "Whatever happens, happens."

"But that scumbag with the weird eyebrows was supposed to give him the clue. He wasn't supposed to take a nap, and he wasn't supposed to start a knife fight. He didn't follow the instructions."

Gavin shrugged. "Bad luck for sure. Everybody knew it wasn't going to be completely fair."

"No, but we can at least get rid of the uncontrolled elements. The drug dealers are actors. Everybody is fine with that. So why not have the crackhead with the clue be an actor, too? Why have so many variables?"

"You're mad because it's your player who's about to get killed."

"I'm not mad, I'm frustrated. And I'm frustrated because it's not necessary. It's stupid to leave so much up to chance."

"I guess you should have chosen a more reliable crackhead."

"I picked somebody within the parameters that I was given."

"Hey, I agree with you," said Gavin. "I'm not the one you should be bitching at. Maybe everybody else is having the same problem."

"Seriously, though, the whole point to this part of the challenge was to see if Ethan would put himself into a dangerous situation to get the next clue. It wasn't supposed to be a knife fight challenge. What kind of jackass would go take a nap and then make a knife fight part of the deal?"

"A drug addicted jackass, presumably."

"I want to punch something," said Rick.

"Go punch Butch."

"Screw you," said Butch.

"Look," said Gavin, "if you're really bent out of shape about this, go ahead and make the call. We all know what they're going to say, but at least you tried."

"You know what? I'm going to do that. Maybe they'll listen to reason."

They had a separate phone that was just for communicating with the people in charge. Rick made the call and put it on speaker.

"Sounds like it's going badly," said The Claw Man. The guys in charge all had stupid-ass nicknames, though Rick did not share his opinion of these nicknames with his employers.

"It's a disaster. I'd like permission to get him out of there."

"No."

"They're going to kill him."

"The danger is real."

"It's not the way the challenge was supposed to work."

"And that's part of the fun of the game. It's unpredictable.

You bribed a psychopath to hand over a clue and it went sideways. You do *not* have permission to pull him out of there. It plays out the way it plays out. Clean up the mess afterward."

"There's a house full of witnesses."

"They're druggies. Pay them off. A thousand bucks each to keep their mouth shut. If they're the ones who killed him, it's win-win for them. Lose-lose for you and Ethan, but it's a game. Most of the players are going to lose."

"All right," said Rick. "I disagree with this but I'll accept your ruling."

"I'll send you a comment card. Bye."

"I told you," said Gavin.

"Maybe he'll surprise you and get out of this," said Butch.

A MAN with a purple scalp (apparently he'd dyed his hair but then shaved his head) pointed a gun at Ethan. "Want me to do it?" he asked almost everybody in the room. Presumably he wasn't seeking Ethan's opinion.

"Hell yeah!" shouted the woman who'd been on Ethan's lap.

"No, dude, don't!" said another guy. "We don't want cops showing up here to investigate the gunshots! We don't want them getting all up in our business!"

The purple-scalped man lowered his gun.

Ethan swung the meat cleaver back and forth in the air, slowly making his way toward the door.

"He can't stop all of us!" said the woman.

"She's right," said Ethan. "But I can take out a couple of you! Does somebody want to lose a hand?" Ethan wasn't sure if he could actually lop off somebody's hand with the meat cleaver, but he was pretty sure none of them knew, either. "You'll win in the end, but whoever comes at me first will get seriously fucked up. Is it worth it?"

He continued moving toward the door. Nobody indicated whether or not they thought it was worth it, but the fact that nobody was currently rushing toward him was a good sign.

"I'm obviously not going to call the cops," he said. "I just want to leave."

He kept slashing at the air with the meat cleaver, not sure if he looked intimidating or ridiculous. Finally he reached the front door and opened it. Nobody made a move as if they were going to stop him.

Ethan kept the meat cleaver with him as he stepped outside, figuring that petty theft was no big deal when a man was bleeding out on the floor.

Tammy wasn't in the car. Big surprise. But at least his car was still there.

He ran to the car, his relief at getting out of there far outweighing his fear over what might happen since he'd failed to obtain the clue, and really had no opportunity to get it now.

As he started the car, he felt an explosion of emotion building up...but, nope, he had to choke that down for right now. Keep it together. He wasn't out of this mess yet, not by any stretch of the imagination.

He sped away from the house.

15

Rick called less than thirty seconds after he drove away. Ethan wondered if he'd been keeping tabs on what was happening in the crack house, or if he was just watching the car.

"I didn't get the clue," said Ethan. "Everything went to crap in there. It could not have gone worse."

"I know," said Rick.

"Did you see it?"

"I'm aware of what happened, yes."

Ethan was trying to keep himself from having a cardiac arrest, but that was an interesting answer. *I'm aware of what happened, yes.* Why not just say yes? Was he admitting that he didn't have hidden cameras in the house?

"What did you see?" Ethan asked.

Rick hesitated for a split second. Just enough to make it clear he had to think about his answer. "That's not a question for you to ask. I know that you accidentally killed the man who was supposed to give you the clue."

"Yeah, because he made us battle with butcher knives and meat cleavers! Was that part of the game?"

"I'm not answering that type of question."

"Does what happened invalidate this round?"

"I wish it did," said Rick.

"So I'm going to have a coke dealer coming after me now?"

"You should go home and get some sleep."

"Are you out of your mind? You think I'm going to go home and go back to bed as if nothing happened? What the hell's the matter with you? For all I know, the cops are on their way to my house right now."

"They aren't."

"Oh, sure, you're a guy I can trust!"

"I've never lied to you," said Rick. "I've withheld information as part of the game but I haven't lied. And because I can tell you're extremely emotional right now, I'm going to assure you that you can go home, take a relaxing shower, and get some sleep."

"Why would I believe you?" asked Ethan. "Seriously, Rick, why would I believe you?"

"Don't do anything stupid. I'll call you before you get home."

RICK CALLED The Claw Man again. "What?" his boss asked, sounding annoyed.

"Ethan's a flight risk," said Rick. "I think he's going to go home, pick up his family, and flee. Or else he'll call the police. We have a completely unstable situation happening right now."

The Claw Man sighed. "All right. End it."

"You mean this challenge?"

"You know perfectly well what I mean. End his game. Terminate him."

"No," said Rick. "If we're going to be so damn concerned with the integrity of the game, we can't kill him just because of what I think he's going to do. He hasn't done it yet. By the guidelines we've established, he doesn't get penalized until he breaks the rules."

"You just said we have a completely unstable situation."

"We do. So we need to stabilize it. We have to fix it, not end his game."

"You're acting like you'll get executed if he loses."

"I'm not concerned with whether my player wins or loses," said Rick. "I'm concerned with what's fair. I'd rather figure out a way to stop him from violating the rules than have to clean it up later, or kill him prematurely."

The Claw Man sighed again, longer and louder this time. "It sounds to me like you made a bad choice with your player."

"I disagree. I made a bad choice with the crackhead. If I'd been able to do a full psychological profile on him before I gave him a hundred bucks to give Ethan an address, I'd have chosen somebody different."

"How are you proposing we course-correct this?"

"The players don't know how the points work, right? None of them have been told."

"Correct."

"So we tweak the rules. We tell Ethan that he can give up a

point in exchange for bypassing a failed challenge. The whole idea of the briefcase filled with cocaine gets thrown out."

"Do you think that will be enough to keep him in line?" The Claw Man asked.

"I'll make sure it is."

"We'd have to offer that option to the other players, too."

"Great! What's wrong with that? I think it's a solid addition to the rules. Shouldn't we try to keep strong players in the game longer?" asked Rick.

"See, now this is where I'm starting to question your motive. Ethan wussed out on the $100,000 broken arm challenge. He failed to save the woman in the grave. So you're not going to convince me that we'd be losing an all-star player here."

"That's a fair comment," said Rick. "That's totally fair. But isn't it better to keep players rather than lose them? We're not lowering the stakes, technically, we're just not letting one moment of bad luck destroy their chances. And we wouldn't let them do it more than once. So if you, say, had three points, you couldn't get a free pass on three different challenges. I honestly think that if this idea had come up in the planning stage, everybody would've been on board with it."

Gavin walked over to the phone. "Hey, Claw Man, it's Gavin. I'll say that I agree with Rick. It's not a bad idea."

They both looked over at Butch.

"Yeah, hey, it's Butch. I like the idea, too."

"Well," said The Claw Man, "your consensus doesn't mean much to me since you're all on Team Ethan. We do it for him, we have to do it for everybody. Harry in Tampa just got shot four times. How is this new rule fair to Harry?"

"He's not dead yet," said Rick. "He can use a point on the

next round. I mean, he'll probably fail at the next challenge if he's been shot four times. It's not completely fair, no, but this is our first play-through. We're still discovering new things. We're working out bugs."

"You call it a bug. I call it a feature."

"C'mon. Let's do it. It'll make the game more interesting."

"You know what, I think you might be on to something," said The Claw Man. "But I can't make the final ruling on my own. I'm going to make a couple of calls, and we'll put it to a vote. Sound good?"

"What if he calls the police before then?"

"Then you kill him and his family."

"All right."

"It'll take two minutes. Talk to you then." The Claw Man hung up.

Rick called Ethan back. "I think I've worked out a solution to your problem," he said. "I just need you to trust me and stay calm."

"Oh, sure, I'm totally calm. Never been calmer. Other drivers keep flagging me down because they want to compliment me on my calmness."

"You sound like you're having a nervous breakdown, and that's completely understandable given the circumstances. But what I really need you to do is trust me, and trust that if you break the rules, you and your family will be punished. You saw for yourself what happens. If you think they'll draw the line at shooting children, you are giving yourself a dangerous false sense of security."

"You think I have a sense of security right now?" Ethan asked, his voice cracking like a teenager going through puberty.

"All I'm saying is, don't do anything stupid."

"Fine. I won't do anything stupid from this point forward."

"Thank you."

Two minutes later, The Claw Man hadn't called him back.

Another two minutes passed.

"Should I call him?" Rick asked Gavin.

"I wouldn't."

"They understand that this is an emergency, right? We're not just sitting around playing cards."

"What are you going to do if you don't like the answer?" asked Gavin.

"Then I'm going to hope that Ethan doesn't do anything stupid before the actors playing drug lords show up to shoot him in the arms and legs."

"Hey," said Butch. "Just got word that the junkies all happily took the bribe and the body is already gone. That chick Tammy got spooked and ran off before Ethan came out, but they caught her and put a bullet in the back of her head. So, go teamwork!"

The other phone rang. Finally!

"I've got some good news for you," said The Claw Man. "I shared your proposal, and believe it or not, it got unanimous approval. Well done."

"Great," said Rick. "Great to hear. Thank you."

"And...now I've got some bad news for you."

"What?"

"We all loved your idea. It will be incorporated into the next game. But we all agreed that it wasn't fair to start it mid-game, when another player has already suffered the consequences for failing to complete the same challenge. So the answer is yes, and you'll get credit for the idea, but the rule change won't go into effect until next time."

"What about Ethan?" Rick asked.

"What about him? We have a protocol in place. We want to discourage it as much as possible, but a player breaking the rules is part of the game. Handle it appropriately. Do you need anything else?"

"No."

The Claw Man hung up.

"What do you think?" asked Gavin. "Think Ethan will get himself and his family all shot up?"

"I'm going to be optimistic and say no."

"He's freaking out," said Butch. "You could hear it in his voice. He's not thinking straight. Twenty bucks says he runs."

"With or without his family?" asked Gavin.

"With. I mean, he's not a douchebag."

"I'll take that bet. What about you, Rick? Want to get in on it?"

"For twenty bucks?" asked Rick. "That's not worth the time to shake your hands."

He called Ethan again.

"How are you holding up?" Rick asked.

Ethan let out an incredulous laugh. "Is that a real question?"

"I'm not suggesting that you should feel particularly sane right now. I just wanted to make sure you were still of sound enough mind to know that you should keep playing by the rules."

"Yes," Ethan told him. "I'm sane enough not to do anything that'll make you send your goons after me."

"I'm glad to hear it."

"I have to go now," said Ethan. "I'm pulling into my driveway right now, but of course you already know that. I'll see if I can fool my family into thinking that I'm not getting back from having slashed some guy's throat."

"I have faith in you."

Ethan hung up. He pulled into his driveway. He left the phone in his car as he went inside. Jenny wasn't in bed—she was sitting on the couch, so that would save time.

"You get Patrick and I'll get Tim," he said. "We're leaving now. Don't even take the time for them to get a change of clothes. Grab your purse and that's it."

Jenny nodded and stood right up. They hurried down the hall and went into separate bedrooms.

Ethan crouched down next to Tim and shook him. Waking him up for school every morning was an extremely difficult task, but there was no time to waste right now. When Tim groaned, Ethan shook him even harder.

"Tim, buddy, get up. Now. Let's go."

"What time is it?"

"Doesn't matter. Get up."

"I'm asleep."

"Get up, Tim. Now!" Ethan grabbed his son's arm and yanked him up.

"Ow! Okay!" Tim got out of bed. He was wearing underwear and a t-shirt instead of pajamas, but he'd just have to ride in his underwear for now. The time spent grabbing something out of his dresser drawers could be the difference between getting out of here before Rick realized what was happening.

Ethan and Tim entered the hallway just as Jenny and Patrick emerged from his bedroom. The four of them ran into the living room and out the front door.

"What's going on?" Patrick asked.

"I'll tell you as soon as we're on the road," said Ethan. "Let's go, let's go, let's go!"

They all got into the car. Ethan looked around. There was no immediate sign that anybody was coming toward the house. He started the engine, backed out of the driveway at a dangerous speed, then drove off.

"You're getting a call," said Jenny, picking up Ethan's phone.

He took the phone from her and answered.

"What the fuck are you doing?" Rick demanded. "I was trying to help you!"

"I decided to help myself."

"Ethan, turn the car around. What are you doing? This is how you die."

"I'm hanging up now."

"No! Don't you dare hang up! We may still be able to salvage this."

"Not interested."

"You'll never make it to the police station. You know that, right?"

"I guess we'll find out."

"Do you think we didn't anticipate something like this?" Rick asked. "Do you think there wasn't a contingency plan? You're going to get Jenny, Patrick, and Tim killed. Your whole family is going to die and it will be your fault."

"I'm done talking," Ethan told him.

"There are explosives attached to the underside of your car. I can set them off with the push of a button. Stop the car *immediately* or you'll leave me no choice."

Rigging Ethan's car to blow up was totally in character for Rick and his associates.

It could also be a desperate bluff.

Quite honestly, blowing up and dying instantly might be a better option than continuing to play this game. Just end it all now.

Ethan rolled down his window.

"What's he saying?" Jenny asked.

"Nothing," Ethan told her.

"You have three seconds," said Rick. "Stop the car in three seconds or I detonate the explosives. I really don't want to do this."

Ethan's foot hovered above the brake pedal.

"I don't believe you," he said, flinging his phone out the window.

16

Had three seconds elapsed?

Even if Rick started counting after he was done talking, it had been three seconds, right?

He didn't want to blurt out "I love you," because that was the kind of thing you said when you thought you were all going to die in a car explosion, and the words wouldn't really matter if they all died an instant after he said them, and if the car *didn't* explode, it might be better if Jenny, Patrick, and Tim didn't know that he was calling a bluff with their lives.

But the car hadn't exploded.

He was still speeding down the street.

Throwing his phone out the window didn't mean Rick wasn't still tracking him or listening in—and in fact it would've been smarter for them to flee in Jenny's vehicle, but he'd been focused on nothing else but getting them out of there as soon as possible. Now that they were potentially out of immediate danger, he'd have to try to make the best strategic decisions going forward.

"You...threw your phone out the window," said Patrick.

"Yes," said Ethan. "I did."

"Who don't you believe?"

"I'm sorry I scared you all," said Ethan. "Daddy has—" Daddy? It had been a long time since "Daddy" was used by anybody in their household. He was definitely losing his mind. "I have a lot to tell you."

"We're listening," said Jenny.

GAVIN AND BUTCH were both staring at Rick. He didn't like it.

He set his phone down on the table. Tried to force a smile. "Well, that could have gone better."

"You think this is a joke?" asked Gavin, standing up.

"No. I do not. I'm sorry."

"You *never* make a threat you can't back up. We had that hammered into us again and again. We never, *ever* give them the chance to call a bluff. Why the hell would you tell him that you could blow up his car? What were you thinking?"

"I wasn't thinking," Rick admitted. "It was a mistake."

"Now he knows that you can't back up your threats."

"I get that," said Rick. "I'm aware of what I've done. It was a major blunder and I apologize."

"Well, don't apologize to me," said Gavin. "I can't believe you did that. That was Game Rules 101. No threats you can't back up."

"I get that!" Rick shouted. "Quit saying the same shit over and over! I messed up! You don't need to keep talking about it!"

"We need to let him know," said Butch.

"Let who know?" asked Rick.

"Who do you think? The Claw Man."

Rick violently shook his head. "No, no, no, let's figure this out first."

"Oh, hell no," said Butch. "We're not going to get in trouble for what you did."

"I'm not asking you to take any of the heat. I'm asking you to hold off bringing in anybody else until we work out how to handle this. We don't know yet what Ethan is going to do. I might still be able to persuade him to see reason."

"Not a chance," said Butch. "This is all on you. I'm not going to let you make it worse for us."

Rick had a gun strapped to his leg.

If he threatened Butch with it, he might be able to convince him not to call anybody quite yet.

Of course, Butch and Gavin also had guns strapped to their legs.

It would be two against one.

He didn't know how long he could hold them off. There was a reason he wasn't part of the team that did things like kill players for breaking the rules.

Since this whole disaster was because of Ethan calling his bluff, he needed to not bluff in this moment. He needed to act.

He pulled out his gun and shot Butch in the forehead.

Well, he *aimed* at Butch's forehead. Even though they were in the back of a van together and it should have been an effortless shot, he actually hit him in the shoulder. There was a lot of blood but it was nowhere close to a kill shot.

Butch cried out in pain as Gavin knocked the gun out of Rick's hand.

Rick was no fighter. But this was life or death and as the adrenaline surged, he grabbed Gavin by the collar and slammed him down onto the table as hard as he could, hoping his face would just splatter.

It didn't.

Gavin pulled away from him. Rick reached for him again. Though Butch was probably going for his own gun, Rick had to worry about the closer problem first.

Rick grabbed Gavin's arm, but Gavin yanked it away.

Butch howled as blood spurted from his bullet wound. Rick had shot him in the right shoulder, and Butch was right-handed, so he was trying to grab for his gun with his left hand, which was costing him time.

Rick dove at Gavin. This was not going to be a graceful fight.

He tried to claw at Gavin's eyes, but Gavin turned his head away, and Rick's neatly trimmed fingernails scraped down his cheek. Rick punched him in the neck. Then he slammed Gavin's head into the table again. Tapping into animalistic rage and survival instinct seemed to be working out pretty well.

He slammed Gavin's head against the table once more. This time the edge of the table bashed into his ear, which had to *really* hurt.

"Get out of the way!" Butch shouted at Gavin. He'd retrieved his gun.

Rick lifted Gavin, trying to use him as a human shield. Gavin was not interested in being used this way, and frantically tried to twist himself out of the way so that Butch could shoot Rick. As they struggled, they bashed into the table, and then they bashed into the other wall of the van.

"Shoot him!" Gavin shouted.

Butch fired.

Rick was not the only person to make a very poor decision. Butch, still spurting blood from his shoulder and obviously not thinking clearly, heeded Gavin's request even though Rick and Gavin were still stumbling around the van. The shot struck Gavin in the very ear that Rick had bashed into the table.

Gavin fell.

Butch took a moment to say "Oh shit!" and gape at what he'd done. That gave Rick time to shoot him in the throat.

Rick said "Oh shit!" and gaped at what he'd done, but since Gavin and Butch were dead, he had that moment to spare.

This was bad. This was so unbelievably bad. He didn't know what kind of punishment he would have received for the botched car bomb bluff—he might have just been severely reprimanded. Or he might have been executed. Right now, standing there staring at the dead bodies and all of the blood, Rick thought that maybe he should have just let them call The Claw Man.

It was obviously too late to take any of this back. Maybe he wasn't completely boned.

The van itself was not monitored, at least as far as Rick knew. He, Butch, and Gavin gave frequent updates, but it didn't necessarily matter which of the three made the call. Nobody would have reason to suspect that he'd just murdered his co-workers. So if he could get Ethan under control, he might be able to put a bandage on this situation until he could run off to South America or something.

The phone on the table rang. The Claw Man was calling.

Ethan wasn't sure how thorough of a confession to give. He decided that leaving out important elements like watching the other player get shot to death and the old woman getting smothered might come back to bite him later, so he gave an almost-complete recap of the events that happened after he walked into the casino. He left out the offer to enjoy physical pleasure with the woman in the crack house, since he saw no particular advantage to Jenny possessing knowledge of that event. And he elected not to traumatize Patrick and Tim by telling them that he'd told their mother about the game during feigned intercourse.

"You made that all up, right?" Patrick asked.

"Do you really think I'd wake you up in the middle of the night and speed off like this as a joke?" It was, admittedly, more credible than the truth. "No, I didn't make it up."

"Holy shit," said Tim.

"I'll allow that one because of the circumstances," said Ethan. "But watch your mouth."

"What are we going to do?" Patrick asked.

"We're going to drive for a while, and then we're going to try to trade out this car in case they're tracing it. Then we'll go to the police."

"But you killed somebody," said Tim.

This was a big part of the conversation that he didn't want to have in front of his children. Suggesting that they shouldn't call the police because Dad accidentally slashed some guy's throat with a meat cleaver would not be setting a good example for the boys. But also, even with the insane circumstances surrounding Grendie's death, he'd be looking at some prison time for manslaughter, right?

He would almost certainly go to the police, and soon, but not necessarily right at this particular moment.

"For now, all I care about is getting you boys and your mom someplace safe," said Ethan. "We'll work out everything else after that."

"We'll get through this," said Jenny. She looked back at the boys. "We'll get through this," she repeated.

They drove in silence for a moment.

"You never get to ground me again," said Patrick.

"I know, smartass."

"I can cheat on tests and do drugs and get girls pregnant and do arson and vandalism and pretty much whatever."

"What's arson?" asked Tim.

"Setting fires on purpose."

"Oh, yeah, I want to do that too."

"You're forgetting something very important," said Jenny. "Your dad may be in the doghouse for the rest of your childhood, but I'm not, and I have equal say in your punishments. So your free pass has just been revoked."

"Shit," said Tim. "I mean, shoot."

Jenny turned back to Ethan. "But we will get through this. We'll figure out a way."

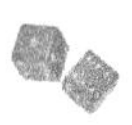

"Hi," said Rick, trying to keep his voice steady.

"Why is his car moving but his phone isn't?" asked The Claw Man.

Rick decided that he should stick to as much of the truth as possible. "He's running. He flipped out over the idea that the drug dealers were going to visit his family and he violated the rules."

"And you guys are on it?"

"We sure are."

"Keep me updated."

"I will."

Rick hung up. That was easier than he'd expected. Now to get in touch with Ethan.

JENNY TOOK OUT HER PHONE. "I'm getting a call from an unknown number," she said.

Ethan's first instinct was that she should fling the phone out the window, but he decided to go with his second instinct, which was to find out who was calling. "Answer it."

"Hello?" she said. She frowned, then handed the phone to Ethan. "It's for you."

"Yeah?" he answered.

"It's me," said Rick.

"I thought I said that I don't want to talk to you."

"I got that. But we can help each other."

"Is that so?"

"We have plans, and backup plans, and backups for our backup plans," said Rick. "If a player goes to the police, we have to enact what we call the Nuclear Option, which sucks. Until that line is crossed, there's still the potential to work something out."

"How do we work it out?" Ethan asked.

"I need you to go back home and pretend you're still playing."

"If I go back home, you'll kill me."

"No. Going back home is your only chance of staying alive."

"I don't believe you."

"In the preliminary rounds, you left with sixty thousand dollars. That was nothing to the people running the game. If you'd won an extra hundred thousand dollars, they wouldn't have blinked. If you'd seen that game through to the end, the final prize would have been one million dollars. A drop in the bucket. And that's just the potential payout to you. This is all a fun game to them, but if they need to, they've got the resources to make problems disappear. Do you think that if the police raided my office in Las Vegas, they'd find the arm-breaking machine? They know how to cover their tracks. I know that you don't believe me, and I completely understand, but there is no happy ending for you unless you trust me."

"I'm not going home," said Ethan. "I'll meet you somewhere to talk in person. If my wife doesn't hear from me in the time that she and I agree on, she's going straight to the FBI and she's telling them everything."

"I'll agree to that," said Rick.

"There's a McDonalds on Eastman Avenue. Call me when you get there. If you keep me waiting too long, the deal is off."

"How long do I have?"

"I'd get right on the road if I were you." Ethan hung up.

"What now?" Jenny asked.

"I'm going to drop you guys off someplace public," Ethan told her, not wanting to say the name of the place out loud.

"Lots of people around. Don't talk to anybody. Don't leave until I call you."

"You threw your phone out the window."

"Right. I did. I still think it was a good idea. I'll call you from Rick's phone."

"Are you sure about this?"

"Not really. But if there's a chance we can work this out, it's better than driving across the country and hoping they don't come after us." He looked at Patrick and Tim in the rearview mirror. "I need you all to take care of each other, okay?"

His sons both silently nodded. Ethan had no idea how he was going to make this up to them.

17

Rick left the dead bodies of Gavin and Butch behind in the van. At some point very soon he'd have to figure out how to get rid of them and explain their disappearance, but for now he'd deal with one apocalypse at a time.

A short while later he pulled into the McDonald's parking lot and called Ethan on his wife's phone. Jenny answered.

"Go to Dorian's Ice Cream," she said. "It's two minutes away. Don't be longer than two minutes."

Rick put Dorian's Ice Cream into his GPS and quickly drove there. It was a small place in a strip mall, and Ethan was seated at a round table right outside.

"Let's get some ice cream," said Ethan, as Rick got out of his car. "Your treat."

They each got double scoop ice cream cones (dark chocolate and peanut butter for Rick, peach and strawberry for Ethan) and returned to the outdoor table.

"This is good," said Rick, tasting his ice cream.

"They make it on site."

"Nice. So let me be blunt, Ethan. The best way for you to stay alive is to keep playing."

"You've said that, but I don't buy it. This game sucks. You keep threatening my family. I'm here to let you try to convince me not to run to the police, but it's not going to be an easy sell."

"I understand. As I said before, if you go to the police, we have to go with the Nuclear Option. There's only so long the authorities can protect you. Best case scenario, I guess, you get your family into a witness protection program, completely uproot your life and start over, but the people running this game are *extremely* rich and they have a lot of free time. They'll find you. The longer it takes, the worse it'll be when they do. I don't think I need to get into the graphic details. Let's just say that when they find the four of you, you'll be the last to go."

"I get what you're saying," said Ethan. "But as you may recall, apparently some scary drug dealers have been told that I stole a briefcase of cocaine from them. If they show up to my house wanting it back, I'm not sure I'm any better off than if I just flee."

"You're better off because..." Rick cleared his throat. "I may have gone a little rogue. Which means that you have somebody on the inside who's sympathetic to your plight. I can give you information. Increase your odds of success."

Ethan took a lick of his ice cream cone. "Give me an example."

"They aren't real drug dealers. They're actors."

"Are you kidding me?"

"Let me be very clear—they're still dangerous. They'll behave the way real-life angry drug dealers would behave in this scenario. We want the game to be as real as possible, but stealing an actual briefcase full of cocaine from actual drug dealers and framing you for it would've been too difficult and unpredictable."

"But you're saying that I'll still have homicidal actors coming to my house?"

Rick nodded. "Not technically homicidal, but yes. The thing is, nowhere in the rules does it say you have to sit back and take it. You're not allowed to go to the authorities. You're not allowed to tell anybody you're in this game. You *are* allowed to take steps to defend yourself. I can give you a number to call where you can hire a couple of men to make this particular problem go away."

"Are you telling me to hire hit men?"

"No. I'm suggesting it."

"How has my life gotten to the point where I'm talking about hiring hit men?"

"They're not cheap, but the money you won in the arm-breaking challenge will cover it. They'll kill the actors quickly and quietly, and take the bodies away. You don't have to do a thing."

"Sounds like they offer top-notch service. So what's an appropriate tip for a professional assassin? Fifteen percent or twenty?"

"Would you like the number or not?" Rick asked.

"Yes, I would. Thank you."

"I'm going to help you as much as I can. If you're willing to work with me and play along, we may be able to get through to the end of the game."

"Okay," said Ethan. "I have a pretty good bullshit detector, and I think you're being honest with me. I'm not saying we won't run off again, but I'll go home for now."

"Perfect."

"Thanks for the ice cream."

"Anytime."

"Can I borrow your phone to call Jenny?"

ETHAN PICKED up Jenny and the kids, then parked at a different restaurant next door. Patrick and Tim stayed in the car while Ethan and Jenny got out to talk. Their children needed to be kept more or less in the loop of what was going on, but the discussion of hiring hit men seemed to belong in the "less" category.

"How'd it go?" Jenny asked.

"I think I have to trust him. He's promised to feed me inside information so I can get through the next challenges. We should go home and play along."

"What about the people coming to kill us?"

"Yeah. We should talk about that. It turns out they aren't real drug dealers, they're actors pretending to be drug dealers, but they're every bit as deadly. Rick gave me a number I can call to hire somebody to make that problem, uh, stop being a problem."

"He told you to hire a hit man?" Jenny asked.

"Yes."

Jenny said nothing for a very long time.

"Do you think we should do it?" she finally asked.

"Maybe."

"How much does something like that cost?"

"A lot. It will probably wipe out most of the money I won."

"Do we want to spend that much?"

"I don't know," said Ethan. "I mean, I guess we could comparison shop."

"What I mean is that we're in a terrible situation right now," said Jenny. "Worst-case scenario, we'll need—well, no, the worst case scenario is we all die. Second worst-case scenario is we'll have to pay somebody for new identities. Even if it doesn't go quite that far, we may desperately need that money to keep ourselves alive."

"I understand that. But we have a more pressing concern than buying new identities."

Again, Jenny said nothing for a very long time.

"Should we pay somebody to do something we can do ourselves?" she asked.

"Excuse me?"

"You barely know Rick. We don't know if the men he'd recommend are any good or not. When the people show up, why not fix the problem ourselves?"

"We don't have a gun."

"We have an axe."

"We have an axe?"

"In the shed."

"Why do we have an axe?" Ethan asked.

"You were going to start cutting firewood."

"I don't remember that."

"It was a long time ago."

"I'm not prepared to fight off somebody with an axe."

"It wouldn't be you," said Jenny. "I'd do it. While they're distracted by you, I'd take them by surprise."

"Let me make completely sure I understand what you're saying," said Ethan. "You're saying that you're willing to kill some actors with an axe?"

"How dedicated are they?"

"I don't know."

"If they take an axe to the leg, do you think they'll stick to the plan?"

"I honestly don't know. I guess not. I wouldn't."

"I don't *want* to do this," Jenny clarified. "I'm only thinking about the future."

"Oh, no, no, I totally get it. It's just, I mean, it's obviously kind of dangerous."

"Extremely dangerous, I assume."

"Right."

"You came home and shouted at us to get out of bed immediately, no time to grab even a change of clothes, and we ran straight for the car to drive out of town. So we're already in a dangerous situation. We might as well try to take control now, so that when we're fleeing for our lives we're at least fleeing with some money in our bank account."

"That does make sense."

"We'll have to improvise," said Jenny. "But I'll have an axe ready, and when they show up, I'll try to make them go away."

Ethan hated, hated, hated this idea, but he had to admit that it seemed like the smartest move right now. Unless the actors killed Jenny, in which case he'd retroactively decide that it was the worst idea of all time. But for now, it seemed like the best move.

NOBODY CALLED as Rick drove back to where he'd left the van and the bodies. That was good. The less communication he had with his boss, the better. They probably wouldn't have anticipated where Rick murdered his co-workers, so they wouldn't be suspicious if they only spoke with him for a while.

When he turned onto the street where he'd left them behind, his stomach plunged.

The van was gone.

Stolen? Towed away? Removed by the Cleanup Crew?

All three of those scenarios were pure disaster.

Actually, every single scenario in which the van with the dead bodies was missing was a terrible one. This was so bad. This was "Why not just shove the barrel of the gun into your mouth and pull the trigger?" bad.

He remembered when working on this game had seemed like the ultimate dream job.

Much of his role involved problem solving, but how could he possibly solve this one? Unless somebody drove up in the van, apologized for accidentally taking the wrong vehicle, and assured him that they hadn't bothered to look in the back, he was one hundred percent screwed.

His phone rang. His stomach somehow hurt even more when he saw that it was The Claw Man. He'd just have to give an Academy Award worthy performance in convincing his boss that everything was simply delightful.

"Hello," Rick said. He hadn't vomited immediately after speaking, so this conversation was off to a good start.

"Just checking in."

"It's all good. I convinced Ethan to return home with his family."

"And you're sure he's actually doing it?"

"Yes. I'm not saying he won't change his mind and do something stupid, but for now I think the situation is under control."

"Good to hear, good to hear," said The Claw Man. "And what about you, Rick? You were sounding a bit stressed out when we last spoke. I was starting to get a little concerned about your well being."

"I'm fine now. I apologize for that. It won't happen again."

"Oh, no need to apologize. You're under a lot of pressure and as your employer I should recognize that. So it's really me who should be apologizing to you. I'm sorry."

It really felt like The Claw Man was just toying with him, but Rick didn't want to give up quite yet in case he was wrong. "Anyway, it's all good."

"And how are Butch and Gavin? This must be stressful for them, too."

Now Rick was starting to feel as if he was passing a kidney stone. "They're fine."

"I'm very glad to hear it. I worry about those guys. It's a relief to know that everything is fine with them. No need to let me talk to them myself—I trust you. What about the van? How's the van doing? Is the van fine, too?"

Rick wanted to collapse to the ground. He had nothing to brace himself against as he felt the dizzy spell come on.

He opened his mouth to speak. He may have made some sort of noise but couldn't be sure.

"Answer my question," said The Claw Man. "How is the van?"

"I—"

"You what? I'm waiting."

"I had to do it."

"You had to do it? Wow. That's not the impression I got at all. I guess I just wasn't paying very close attention as I watched you murder the two men you were supposed to be working with. From my perspective, it was a decision you made on your own. Explain to me how I'm wrong."

Rick couldn't talk.

"I know we told you that the van and your other working spaces weren't monitored," said The Claw Man. "We were fudging the truth, and wondering if you'd be stupid enough to believe it. Of course we're monitoring you. We want to know everything that happens. That's part of the fun."

Rick still couldn't force himself to speak.

"We worked out a lot of different hypothetical scenarios, but I'll be honest, we never considered that our employees would start killing each other. That was a bit of a shocker. We'll know for next time, I guess."

"Sir—"

"You don't have to call me sir. We're not suddenly more formal around here. I know you're probably waiting for a bullet to blow the back of your head apart, and it's a legitimate concern. I'd be worried about that too. But this is still one big game, and my buddies and I kind of like the idea of making you see this through to the end."

Had Rick heard right? Were they *not* going to kill him?

"You're going to continue to do your job to the best of your ability. But that bullshit where you feed inside information to Ethan to help him win? That's gone. It's gameplay as usual, except that obviously we have to send in replacements for Butch and Gavin. Lucky for you, we've got that covered."

"Thank you," said Rick.

"Don't thank me. I *know* you don't think this is happening without a penalty."

"I don't think that."

"This is the part of the game that I like to call 'raising the stakes.' Congratulations, Rick! You've just become much more invested in this. The new rule is pretty simple: If Ethan loses, you lose. Get it?"

"Yes," said Rick. "I get it."

"I bet you don't. Not completely. When I say that you lose, it's quite a bit more expansive than what you're thinking. You don't get along with your ex-wife Melissa, but you would do anything for your daughter Cynthia. Well, Cynthia loses, too. Your mom and dad, still happy and healthy and living in Arizona? They lose, too. Shall I go on? I think I'll go on. Your fuck buddy, Gwendolyn? She loses. Your other fuck buddy, the married one, Sunny? She loses. Your beloved Uncle Charlie? He loses. The list goes on, but I'm going to guess that your daughter is reason enough for you to take the rest of the game very, very seriously."

"I will," said Rick. "I promise."

The Claw Man chuckled. "I can almost hear the sweat pouring down your face. I'll be honest, the game is a little more fun for me now. I'll be in touch." He hung up.

Rick's legs suddenly couldn't support his weight anymore and he collapsed onto the road.

18

Ethan pulled into his driveway, wondering if this was a mistake that would cost him and his family their lives. Were the people running this game really so powerful that there was nowhere to hide? Or was that just an absurd scare tactic? Was he being a complete idiot by trusting Rick?

For now, he had to assume that he was doing the right thing.

Everybody got out of the car. They silently went into the house, and then he told Patrick and Tim to go to bed, and to lock themselves inside their bedrooms. His sons did so without protest.

Ethan started some prep work that he didn't want to explain out loud, and Jenny went out to the shed to get the axe.

THE VAN HAD BEEN RETURNED to its former spot, minus the bodies of Gavin and Butch. It was weird and uncomfortable for

Rick to sit in here, though at least they'd cleaned up all the blood. The cleanup crew had done a thorough job. True professionals.

Rick wished he could help Ethan cheat, as promised, but he didn't dare. He had to assume that every call, every keystroke, hell, every *thought* was being monitored. He had to play the game completely straight from now on. Which meant that Ethan's odds of making it to the very end were extremely low—perhaps even lower than the other players because Ethan believed he had an unfair advantage and might not try as hard.

The Claw Man called. "The actors just landed," he said, when Rick answered.

"Are we doing it tonight?"

"Yes, they'll head straight over."

"Do they know Ethan knows they're not real drug dealers?"

"No. We decided to let it play out the same as their other visits."

Rick felt a bit of relief. That was good. It still gave Ethan a slight advantage.

"That still gives Ethan an advantage," said The Claw Man. Rick knew he wasn't *truly* reading his mind, but it was unsettling. "We'll have to balance that out in the next challenge."

"I understand."

"Your new partners won't be there until 6:00 AM. So you'll be monitoring this one by yourself, but I hope you're not suicidal enough to think you can get away with anything."

"I'm definitely not suicidal enough for that," Rick assured him.

"Good. Expect them to arrive in twenty minutes."

"I will. Thank you."

Not having Gavin and Butch's replacements in the van with him didn't really offer any special opportunities for Rick, not if the entire van was under surveillance. It just meant less annoying conversation, although to be perfectly honest, annoying conversation was exactly what Rick needed right now to get out of his own head. He could feel himself rocketing toward a nervous breakdown.

Gotta keep it together.

Ethan might surprise him. For now, Rick would go with optimism over nihilism. This all might just work out.

THE DOORBELL RANG.

Ethan immediately got up off the couch and answered. Two men stood outside his front door. They sure as hell *looked* like angry drug dealers, and Ethan found himself taking an unconscious step backward.

"Ethan Caustin?" asked the one who wore a dark blue suit.

Ethan nodded. "What's all this about?"

"May we come in?"

"My family is asleep."

"We'll be quiet."

Ethan stepped out of the way. The men walked into his living room and Ethan shut the door behind them. The second man, who was quite a bit larger than his partner, walked around, surveying their surroundings.

"I think you know why we're here," said the first man. "You have something that belongs to us."

"Right," said Ethan. "I do. Sorry for playing dumb when I

asked what this was all about. Yes, I've got your briefcase. It's right over here." Ethan walked over to the bookshelf and picked up a brown leather briefcase that had been in the back of the closet pretty much since they moved into this home. He handed it to the man. "Here you go."

The man looked confused.

"It's all there," Ethan assured him.

"This isn't my briefcase."

"No, it's not the same briefcase. It's actually a nicer one. But the contents are the same."

"I'm going to have to inspect it."

"Of course. I wouldn't expect you to take my word for it."

The man, still looking confused, set the briefcase on the coffee table in front of the couch. He popped open the latches, then hesitated.

"You open it," he told Ethan.

"Oh, sure, sure." Ethan crouched down next to the latches. "I wish I knew how to booby trap a briefcase. This is the first time I've ever been involved in anything even remotely like this. The first *and* last time, just to be clear. It's a funny story how I accidentally ended up with your briefcase. Do you want to hear it?"

"No. Just open it."

Ethan opened the lid. Inside the briefcase were several plastic bags filled with white powder.

The man and his partner exchanged a glance.

"It's all there," Ethan insisted. "I don't want any of it. I smoked some pot in college but that's as far as it ever went."

"It still looks kind of light," said the man.

It was definitely kind of light. Ethan had used all the sugar, flour, and baking soda they had in the house, but it wasn't close to four and a half kilos. It wouldn't fool anybody who did even the most cursory inspection. Ethan was banking on the idea that these actors would decide that this was good enough.

The man looked unsure what to do. "I need to test it."

"Test away."

He picked up one of the bags. "This is obviously not cocaine," he said. "It's granulated. What is this, sugar?"

"It's sugar, yes," Ethan admitted. "But it's the good stuff."

"Is this a joke?"

"No, it's a role."

"Excuse me?"

"We're both playing roles. You're playing the role of the revenge-minded drug dealer trying to reclaim his product, and I'm playing the role of the family man desperately trying to get out of this mess. This isn't real."

The man held up a pistol. "This gun is sure real."

"True. But the contents of that briefcase are every bit as real as your drug dealer credentials, so why not take it and go? I think we've both given fine acting performances. If you want to make this more real, I promise you, I'm willing to get as real as it takes to defend my family, and it'll get bloody. There'll be blood dripping from the ceiling when we're done. Some yours, some mine. Why let it go that far? If you take the briefcase and leave, you've done your job."

The two actors exchanged another glance.

"I need to make a call," said the one who'd been doing all the talking. He walked out the front door.

The larger man just stared at Ethan.

"Can I get you anything?" Ethan asked.

"Nah."

"Beer?"

The man shook his head. "No, thank you."

They stood there silently.

A minute later, the other man came back inside. He walked over to the coffee table, closed the briefcase, and picked it up. "Okay," he said.

"Okay?" his partner asked.

"Okay." He looked at Ethan. "Thank you for returning our merchandise."

"You're welcome."

The men left.

A moment later, Jenny pushed open the closet door that had been ajar. She leaned the axe against the wall. "Glad I didn't need that."

Rick's mood was far from celebratory, but he was feeling a little better. The lack of bullet wounds, even superficial ones, would give Ethan a better chance in the later rounds.

He called Ethan. "Nice work," he said. "I'm glad Jenny didn't have to use the axe, too."

"What's next?" Ethan asked.

"Get some sleep. Continue your life as usual."

"For how long?"

"Get some sleep," Rick repeated. "Continue your life as usual."

Actually, Ethan and the other players had about three days before the next challenge. This was partly so that the players who'd been less fortunate regarding the briefcase of cocaine had time to heal, and also to test everybody's ability to stay sane as they waited that long for something to happen.

GAVIN AND BUTCH's replacements arrived exactly on time. Their names were Quincy and Tyler and they'd clearly been told exactly why they'd been sent to Kansas City, since they glared at Rick a lot and had no interest in any kind of small talk. Rick was kind of worried to make any sudden moves around them.

Ethan and Jenny both called in sick to work the next day, and they called the school to say their sons were sick. Rick was worried about this, since it was technically a departure from their standard routine, but he couldn't imagine that there was any way Ethan would send Patrick and Tim off to school. Fortunately, The Claw Man didn't have a problem with them staying home, since the players who'd been shot had been encouraged to stay home as well.

The surveillance was extremely tedious, but they couldn't stop being fully attentive. It was simultaneously possible that Ethan would get scared by the long stretch of nothing happening and decide again that they needed to flee, and that he'd feel emboldened by the long stretch and assume they weren't paying as close of attention to him.

But the Caustin family didn't do anything to cause problems. They didn't talk about the game at all. They stayed home and watched a lot of television. Their behavior was perfect. Considering the circumstances, they were handling things very well.

ETHAN THOUGHT he was going to lose his fucking mind.

He didn't *want* to be called for the next challenge, but staying home from work, keeping Patrick and Tim out of school, and being terrified to do anything that might set off a red flag for Rick's bosses was driving him insane. He was proud of Jenny and the kids, but they were unquestionably feeling the strain, and he was frightened that one of them would finally snap.

He'd often thought that it would be so nice to be able to just sit on the couch and binge-watch television shows with no sense of guilt over the stuff he should be doing, but now that he was in this situation, he couldn't enjoy the experience. They might as well have been watching the same episode of the same show over and over, since he wasn't processing any of it.

This went on for three days. He couldn't sleep. He had no appetite. And Rick wouldn't give him any information about how much longer this was going to continue. Was the challenge imminent? Was it a week away? Was this the actual challenge—an endurance test to see how long he could last before he started clawing his own eyes out?

That moment might not be far away.

"IT'S TIME," said Quincy.

"Thank you," said Rick, who knew perfectly well that it was time but who was trying to be as polite as possible to his co-workers. He called Ethan. On his monitor, he saw Ethan lunge for his cell phone.

"Hello?"

"It's time for your next challenge."

"What is it?"

"I can't tell you that. But I can tell you the odds."

"I'm listening."

"You have a one in three chance of winning a fantastic prize. You have a one in three chance of winning a good prize. And you have a one in three chance of incurring a penalty."

"A penalty."

"Right."

"And I don't suppose you're going to tell me what the prizes or penalty is?" Ethan asked.

"I wish I could."

"What do you think I should do?"

"Are you asking for my honest professional opinion?"

"Yes."

"You should do it."

"Okay. Then I accept."

"Great. A van is on the way to pick you up."

"I'll be here."

They hung up. "Are you asking for my honest professional opinion?" had been obvious code for "Do you want the inside scoop that I'm not supposed to share with you?" And technically Rick had given him an honest answer, because he did truly believe that Ethan should accept the challenge in an attempt to win the prizes.

But, God, the penalty was *horrific.*

19

"That was work," said Ethan. "They're on the way to pick me up for another job."

Jenny, Patrick, and Tim all looked very serious and scared. Ethan tried to give them a reassuring smile, though it probably looked more like a grimace.

"I'll be totally fine. I'll let you know when I'm on my way back."

They all got up off the couch. Ethan gave each of them a hug, trying to avoid the vibe that this could be a goodbye hug. He'd be fine. Rick had gone rogue and would make sure this all worked out okay.

He heard a vehicle pull into the driveway and went outside. It was a black van that could not have looked more sinister if it had a scary clown drawn on the side and a sign reading "Free Candy." The side door slid open and Rick got out.

"Good morning," said Rick. "How are you this fine day?"

"Never better." Ethan walked over to the van. "Nothing quite like getting into a black van to make me feel at ease."

Rick chuckled. "It'll be fine. Climb on in."

Ethan got into the van. The driver, who looked old enough to die of natural causes while operating the motor vehicle, glanced back and gave Ethan a polite nod. Nobody else was in there. Ethan sat down and fastened his seat belt as Rick climbed in after him and shut the door.

"Looks like you got screwed," said the driver.

"Why?"

"You're the closest. You got a van instead of a private jet."

"Yeah, that does suck," Ethan admitted.

As they drove off, Rick handed Ethan a phone. "It doesn't have an Internet connection, but you can play games on it. Just to keep you entertained on the way."

"How long is the drive?"

"Not too bad. Six hours."

Ethan sighed. "Am I allowed to just sleep?"

"If you can, sure. Rest up."

Ethan reclined the seat and tried to go to sleep, but of course that was a wasted effort. He tried to play some games on the phone and couldn't focus on any of them. He tried again to sleep, unsuccessfully, and ultimately just settled for staring out the window as Rick immersed himself on whatever he was doing on a laptop computer.

The six hours did not pass quickly.

They stopped at a couple of rest areas for bathroom breaks. Ethan was not given any instructions not to run off, since apparently it wasn't something that needed to be underscored at this point. He used the restroom and dutifully returned to the van.

"Not much further," Rick told him as they pulled off the highway. They drove through a residential area, and then through an area that had more of a post-apocalyptic feel, where roving gangs of mutants would attack you to steal your teeth. Actually, the area just didn't look like many people lived around there—the whole post-apocalyptic thing was added by Ethan's imagination, which was going into some very dark places right now.

They pulled into a very long, winding driveway, finally parking in front of a large yellow house.

"We're the first ones here," said Rick. "That's good. You've got some extra time to stretch your legs."

They got out of the van and went inside the home. It was sparsely furnished and gave the impression of "second home that's not used very often." Rick offered Ethan and the driver a bottle of water from the refrigerator, then they sat on the living room couch.

"Do you want to watch television?" Rick asked.

"Nah, that's all right," said Ethan.

"Can I have the remote?" the driver asked.

Rick handed it over. The driver turned on the television, switched the channel to one of those courtroom shows, and sat back happily on the couch as he watched. Ethan just sat there, wondering when Rick might tell him what kind of advantage he had in the challenge. Maybe it would never be safe to tell him. He'd just have to trust the guy.

After about half an hour of shitty TV, Rick got a call. He said

"Okay" a couple of times, hung up, then stood up. "We're ready to go."

Rick and Ethan went out to the backyard. A wooden fence, not quite as tall as Ethan, blocked everything from view. Five other people were standing there. Ethan had never met any of them, but from the expressions and body language, it was pretty obvious that a blonde woman and a man slightly younger than Ethan were the other two players.

A middle-aged man with an expensive looking haircut and too-white teeth walked over and shook Ethan's hand. He wore a t-shirt with a giant crab claw on the front. "Pleased to finally meet you in person," he said. "It's great to shake the hand of somebody I've been spying on all this time." He laughed. "Ethan, I want you to meet Kenny and Lisa. They'll be your competitors in the next challenge."

Ethan had guessed correctly. He assumed the other two people—a man and a woman—had the same job as Rick.

Lisa only appeared to be in her early twenties, and she looked extremely fit, like she jogged every day without hating every second of it. Kenny had a somewhat doughier body type, but in a one-on-one altercation, Ethan wasn't sure he could take him. He hoped this wasn't too physical of a challenge, and that Rick had taken care of him as promised.

Rick did not look like somebody who was confident that he had everything under control.

"Before I tell you about the challenge," said The Claw Man, "I'll tell you about the prizes." He walked over to a small table, upon which rested a wooden box. He lifted the lid. "To the winner goes this unregistered, untraceable, fully loaded pistol. You'll be glad to have it. Plus, you get a point." He replaced the lid. "To the second place finisher, no weapon, but you also get a point."

"When are you going to tell us what the points are for?" Kenny asked. The man next to him looked annoyed, as if they'd discussed this already.

The Claw Man ignored him. "Now I'm guessing that what you *really* want to know is what penalty the loser receives. So everybody follow me."

The seven of them walked around the perimeter of the fence until they saw a shed. The Claw Man opened the door and gestured inside.

There was large steel barrel, resting upon what appeared to be a giant stovetop burner. Suspended from the ceiling was a pair of chains with handcuffs on the end.

"Inside that barrel is boiling oil," said The Claw Man. "The loser of this challenge will be slowly lowered into the oil—feet first, because we don't want the suffering to end too soon. I assume they'll be dead before they're completely submerged. I'm sure it's not the worst possible way to die, but it's not one of the better ones."

Lisa and Kenny did not drop to their knees and beg for mercy, so Ethan didn't, either.

"Oh, and there's another prize," said The Claw Man. "First place doesn't have to watch. Second place won't be so lucky."

They walked away from the shed and back to where they'd been standing before. The Claw Man opened the gate to the fenced-in area.

"The rules are very simple," he said. "You will run through the maze searching for three keys. Lisa, yours are red. Kenny, yours are green. Ethan, yours are blue. You may not steal somebody else's keys. When you have all of your keys and have come back to the start, you've completed the challenge. Aside from that, all you have to worry about are all of the traps. Any questions?"

Nobody had any questions.

"Ethan, bad news for you, buddy. Because you had an unfair advantage in a previous challenge, we have to balance it out. You will be collecting four keys instead of three."

"I'm sorry, what?" Ethan asked.

"Was I unclear? To win this challenge, you will have to collect four blue keys from inside the maze."

Ethan wanted to protest. Yes, he'd escaped being shot by the fake drug dealers because he'd had inside information, but the penalty there was nowhere near as bad as being slowly lowered into a barrel of boiling oil. He would've taken the gunshots! However, it was very clear that arguing this would be a complete waste of breath.

He looked over at Rick again, hoping for a wink or a hand signal or something, *anything* to make him believe that things were under control. Instead, Rick averted his eyes.

That son of a bitch had completely screwed him over. Ethan should have thrown Jenny's phone out the window as well and just kept driving.

"I asked you a question," said The Claw Man. "Was I unclear?"

"No," said Ethan.

"One last rule. This one's important so everybody listen up. This is a competition, not a team-building exercise. However, if one of you dies inside the maze—and it's entirely possible that this will happen—then the *second*-place finisher goes into the oil.

So don't try to kill each other while you're in there. I wish it didn't have to be said, but there was an incident earlier. Any questions?"

Kenny raised his hand.

"Yes?" The Claw Man asked.

"Can we injure each other?"

The Claw Man thought about that. "Knock yourself out. Or knock them out. You can try to stretch the rules if you want, but don't let it bite you in the ass. Anybody else?"

Ethan and Lisa had no questions. Actually, Ethan had a million questions, but none that he should ask right now.

The Claw Man gestured to the maze. "Everybody step inside. Don't start running yet."

The three players walked into the maze. The walls on the inside were shorter than the fence, but Ethan couldn't see over them. There were five different directions they could go, with the corridors wide enough that two (but not three) players could run side by side.

"Remember, it's not enough to find all of your keys. You must exit the maze here." He took out a gun. "On your mark...get set...*go*!"

He fired the gun into the air.

Kenny shoved Ethan against the wall.

"C'mon!" Kenny said to Lisa. "If we take him out now we can guarantee that we won't lose!"

Lisa shook her head. "You do whatever you want," she said, then she took off running down the far left path.

Kenny's visible disappointment at her rejection of his plan was distraction enough for Ethan to punch him in the jaw. Kenny stumbled backwards and almost went out the open entrance to the maze. He looked as if he were going to lunge at Ethan, then changed his mind and ran down the far right path.

There was merit to the "incapacitate another player" scheme, but instead Ethan ran down the path next to the one Lisa had taken.

It went on for about ten feet, then split into a left or right turn. Ethan took the left one.

Was it safe to be running in a booby-trapped maze?

Possibly not. But surely they wouldn't design it so that he could set off a tripwire that blew his legs off and ended the challenge. Unless the trick to winning was to just wait for the other two players to get killed.

For now, he'd assume that the key was to race through it as quickly as possible.

He took three more turns and continued to see only bare wooden walls.

The Claw Man spoke over a megaphone: "Lisa has just found her first key!"

Already?

Ethan picked up his pace...and then immediately stopped as he made a left turn and saw that the corridor had dozens of knife blades protruding from the walls and floor. This one was much more narrow than the other corridors—no way could two people get through side by side.

This went on for about ten feet. Past that, he thought he could see some multi-colored metallic objects hanging on the wall, which he assumed were the keys. Were the knives here to dissuade him from moving forward? He couldn't tell if this hallway dead-ended or not. There might be a much safer path to the keys, or this might be it.

He decided to go forward. There was enough room to maneuver around the knives as long as he was *extremely* careful.

Ethan turned sideways and stepped down the corridor, moving cautiously but also trying not to fall behind in the race. Though there wasn't much room to spare, as long as he didn't lose his balance he should be able to avoid getting impaled.

He was a quarter of the way through already. See, this wasn't so bad. He could do this.

The corridor seemed to be narrowing a bit.

Yes, the tips of the blades were scraping against him, though not breaking the skin.

Ethan kept moving.

Halfway through. Still going fine.

"Holy shit," said Kenny.

Ethan glanced over. Kenny stood at the end of the hallway, where Ethan had been, looking at the knives without much enthusiasm.

Then, like Ethan, Kenny turned his body sideways and began to move through the bladed corridor.

Ethan kept going.

He winced as a blade tore the back of his shirt.

Another blade tore the front of his shirt.

And suddenly he was feeling claustrophobic.

Ethan kept his focus on the path ahead, even though it sounded like Kenny might be quickly gaining on him. Surely Kenny wouldn't attack him while they were squeezing through the corridor of blades—if Ethan got disemboweled, Kenny would almost certainly be the one to go into the oil.

Now Ethan could see that this corridor did indeed have a dead end. He'd have to go back through the knives again.

The blades were breaking the skin. Not enough that he'd bleed to death or even be slowed down, but they hurt like hell. There really wasn't room for him to contort himself to avoid getting cut. He pretty much had no choice but to just keep going and hope the blades didn't cut too deep.

Kenny was breathing heavily, as if he was starting to panic.

Three-quarters of the way there. Still doing fine.

The blades were now cutting his chest, back, and legs. Still not badly.

At least it wasn't too difficult to avoid the knives protruding from the floor.

Almost there.

One blade across his back cut deeper than the others and he yelped. He allowed himself three seconds to pause and regain his composure before moving again.

He made it. Ethan exhaled deeply, not having even realized he'd been holding his breath. A red, green, and blue key dangled from strings. Ethan took the blue one and shoved it into his pocket.

"Ethan has his first key!" The Claw Man announced.

Kenny had stopped moving. His eyes were squeezed shut and he looked like he was trying to control his panicked breathing.

This was a problem, because there was no way to get past him.

Was Ethan allowed to climb over the wall? Nobody had said it was against the rules. He was far from a star athlete, but surely he could pull himself up and over a wall that was about the same height as he was.

He reached up and grabbed the top of the maze wall.

The Claw Man spoke over the megaphone. "There is no rule

against climbing over the walls. But you will become target practice." A gunshot rang out.

Ethan did not want to become target practice, so he let go of the wall.

"Turn back," he told Kenny.

Kenny didn't open his eyes. "Not a chance."

"I'll bring you your key."

"That isn't allowed."

"They didn't say I couldn't bring you your key. They said I couldn't steal it."

"No. I can't trust you."

"Then at least get moving. Lisa already has one of her keys."

"I'm trying!"

Kenny didn't budge. Ethan couldn't wait here forever, so he turned sideways and moved back into the bladed corridor.

The knives immediately began to cut him, but he knew that this time it would get easier as he went along.

Well, at least it would until he ran into Kenny.

20

s Ethan moved through the bladed corridor, Kenny opened his eyes. Then Kenny began to slowly step toward him.

"Go the other way," Ethan told him.

"I'm not backtracking."

"Do you really want to fight here? It's barely even safe to breathe."

"I'd rather die here than get dunked in boiling oil, so yeah, I'd rather fight you than let you get ahead of me."

"I said I'd get your key for you," said Ethan. "Why not work together? Hell, I can get all of our keys, and all you have to do is keep Lisa from getting past you." It would be a dirty trick, but one of the players was going to die an agonizing death soon, and Ethan felt no guilt over the fact that he really did *not* want it to be him.

"You'll screw me over," said Kenny.

The longer they spent discussing this, the more time Lisa

would have to gather her keys. If Kenny wanted to be an idiot, Ethan wasn't going to play along.

He'd just have to be scary.

"Fine," he said. "Then get the fuck out of my way."

Ethan moved quickly toward Kenny. The blades slashed him as he went. He'd either intimidate Kenny into backing out of the corridor, or shove him out and hope that the gashes he received weren't fatal.

"I'm not kidding," said Ethan. "You'd better fucking move."

Kenny looked unsure for a moment, then began to move the other way.

Ethan didn't slow his pace.

Kenny emerged from the bladed corridor.

Ethan kept going, hoping that Kenny wouldn't attack him before he cleared the knives. He slashed his arm right where he'd cut it during the battle to save the old woman, then finally got out of the corridor. Kenny stepped away to give him room, possibly because Ethan now looked like a blood-covered deranged madman.

"Should've let me get your key," said Ethan, walking past him into a new corridor.

Okay, he now had an advantage because he had his first key and Kenny didn't. But he had to find an extra key, so technically they were on even ground right now.

He took a turn, and then another turn, and then realized that he could easily find himself hopelessly lost. He didn't have breadcrumbs or spray paint, but he did have plenty of leaking blood, so he wiped some blood on the wall before each turn to make sure that he wasn't going in circles.

"Lisa has found her second key," The Claw Man announced. "Only one more left before she wins!"

Ethan couldn't let this distract him. He'd never expected to come in first. He just didn't want to lose.

In the next corridor, there was a large plaid floor mat, with no room to walk around it. Presumably it covered a pit of some sort, so Ethan wasn't going to be dumb enough to simply stroll across it. He crouched down and pulled it up to see what it covered.

It covered scorpions. Lots and lots of scorpions.

They spilled off the bottom of the mat onto his legs.

For an instant Ethan thought that they couldn't be real, but then he realized that they absolutely were. He tossed the mat back onto the ground and frantically brushed the scorpions off his legs.

Before too many of them could climb out of the shallow pit, he backed up a few steps, then did a running jump, clearing the pit, then tumbled forward and crashed to the ground. He quickly got up, hurried around the corner, and almost smacked into the wall. A dead end.

Without hesitation, he ran back the way he came and leapt over the scorpion pit again. It wasn't an Olympic-level jump, but his legs had just been cut up, and the sudden jolt of pain as he left the ground made his leap less impressive than it otherwise might have been. His feet landed on the edge of the pit, and he fell backwards, scorpions crunching underneath his body as he landed.

He got right the hell up and hurried away from the pit.

It was probably worth losing some valuable seconds to make

sure no venomous scorpions were crawling on his body. A few were, so he brushed them off. He could feel the scorpion guts clinging to the back of his shirt, but he didn't think he'd been stung. He briefly considered replacing the mat so that it would slow down Lisa or Kenny, but decided that he didn't have time for that.

He kept running through the maze, still wiping his blood on the wall at each decision point. Thus far he was covering all new territory.

At a fork, he started to go left, but then he saw Lisa run past at the end of the path to the right. She'd already found two of her keys, so he wanted to go where she'd been. He took the path to the right.

At the end of this path, the wall was covered with keys. Hundreds, maybe thousands of them, in a huge array of colors.

Ethan decided to give himself one opportunity to just try to scan the wall for the blue key. If he couldn't find it, he'd go with a more methodical approach.

He slowly walked along the corridor, trying to clear his mind and focus only on finding the color blue. So many keys...

There!

He grabbed a light blue key off its hook and shoved it into his pocket. Then he raced off.

"Ethan has picked up a second key!" The Claw Man announced.

Two down. He was still in this. Maybe Kenny was still paralyzed with fear and would keep Lisa from retrieving her final key.

Despite his many turns, he had yet to come across a wall that was already streaked with his blood. This maze was frickin' huge.

At the next turn, the corridor had a ceiling. Hanging from

the ceiling was a line of about a dozen of what looked like guillotine blades. They were placed at different heights, probably so the closest one wouldn't block the others and the players could see that there were plenty of them.

To get underneath all of them, he wouldn't simply have to crawl—he'd have to lie flat on his stomach and scoot.

Might as well get right to it.

He lay flat on the ground and did his best to move forward. It wasn't the kind of thing somebody should be doing when covered with knife wounds, and he was going to be extremely unhappy if this led to another dead end without a key.

He passed under the first guillotine blade. This process involved a lot of trust that the blade wouldn't drop down and decapitate him, but he had to still go with the idea that the game designers weren't actually trying to kill him. Granted, he'd just fallen onto a bunch of live scorpions, so it was entirely possible that a blade would fall, chop off his hands, and make him feel amazingly foolish as the blood sprayed from his new stumps.

He scooted as quickly as he could, ignoring the pain it was causing.

No guillotine blades had dropped yet.

Now his body was entirely underneath them. The blades could chop him into a dozen sections. He tried to push that thought out of his mind but was completely unsuccessful.

The blade right in front of him dropped.

Suddenly all of the others did as well.

Ethan screamed as all of the blades landed on him...but didn't actually do anything. Though he could feel the metal on the back of his neck, it was too dull to actually slice off his head.

"Good one," he said out loud. "Really amusing."

He lifted the blade in front of him and it went up with little effort. He continued scooting forward. After he cleared the last blade, they all slid back up to their original positions. He got up and continued on his way.

"Kenny has found a key!" The Claw Man announced. Wow. That took forever. And he still had to go back through the bladed corridor.

Sadly, there wasn't another key waiting just beyond the hall of guillotines. But perhaps it was nearby. He'd search the whole area. Too bad he wasted blood on the ground that could've been used to mark the walls.

This time he backtracked a few times to make sure he wasn't going too far from the last trap, but no luck. There was no key around here.

He ran through a hallway that had left turn after left turn after left turn, as if he was running through a spiral. The center of a spiral seemed like a pretty good place to hide a key. When he made it there—nothing. Yet another dead end. He cursed and turned around to run back out of it.

"Lisa has her third and final key!" The Claw Man announced.

Ethan cursed again. That was way sooner than he'd expected. Kenny must have exited the bladed corridor much faster than he'd entered it, and then Lisa zipped right through. This didn't mean complete disaster, since Ethan had felt like he was really just playing for second place anyway, but it would've been nice if Lisa had broken her leg or something.

He kept running.

At the next intersection, he saw a streak of blood. He'd already gone to the left, so he went to the right.

If Kenny or Lisa were bleeding, they could throw him off. He wouldn't worry about that right now.

After a couple more turns, he saw a blue key hanging on the wall. There wasn't a green key next to it, so this must be the extra key he had to find. Ethan grabbed it.

"Ethan has found another key!" The Claw Man announced. And then, a moment later, "Lisa has just exited the maze! Lisa is our winner! Who will come in third and get the boiling oil?"

No need to panic. Ethan was still ahead.

"And the developments just keep coming!" The Claw Man announced. "Kenny has another key!"

Still no need to panic.

Ethan kept going. Thank God he'd thought of the blood trick, because aside from the occasional trap, each part of the maze was starting to look the same. He'd completely lost track of where he was in relation to the maze entrance.

He caught a glimpse of light on the ground ahead and slowed down. A tripwire ran across the corridor. The filament had caught the sunlight, saving him from whatever horrible thing would happen if he snapped the wire. He carefully stepped over it and resumed running.

"Kenny has a third key!" The Claw Man announced.

What the hell? Already? Had Lisa shared information with him?

And were those footsteps ahead of him?

Ethan stopped and listened carefully. Yes, he could hear Kenny running, which meant the key was probably to the left instead of the right. He now knew where it was—he just had to figure out how to get there.

He maneuvered through the maze to where he thought he'd

heard the footsteps. Maybe he was correct, but there was no sign of a key. He raced back to where he'd started and tried a different path. Still no luck. Unless there was an extra person running around, he had to at least be close to the right spot.

Did Kenny know the way out?

Should Ethan start thinking of a contingency plan? Wouldn't it be better to let The Claw Man shoot him for climbing over the wall than to be lowered into the oil?

Nihilism wasn't going to help right now. He'd worry about getting himself killed on purpose *after* he lost the race. For now, he was still in the game.

He took another path, and then rejoiced at the sight of three skulls mounted into the wall. Skulls were not typically a sight that caused him to rejoice, but their mouths were open, and he could see that there was a blue key inside one of them.

The skull jaw might be spring-loaded to snap shut on his fingers. Ethan didn't care.

He grabbed the key and ran.

Now he just had to get out of the maze before Kenny did.

The blood on the walls would tell him where he'd been, but it wouldn't really help him find his way out. Was The Claw Man standing by the entrance when he spoke through the megaphone? That could be a clue.

Ethan ran as fast as he could.

He raced through the maze for a couple of minutes, grateful to not hit any dead ends. He hoped that Kenny wasn't as fortunate.

"Ooooh, it's a nail biter!" The Claw Man announced. "Kenny is almost out!"

Ethan turned left, then right, then hit a dead end.

If The Claw Man was indeed announcing from by the entrance, then Ethan needed to take the huge risk and save himself some time by unleashing his inner gymnast.

He grabbed the top of the wall and quickly pulled himself up.

It hurt, both because he was out of shape and because he was covered in cuts, but he forced himself to climb over the wall as fast as he could.

A gunshot rang out.

It felt like it came *very* close.

Ethan made it over the wall and fell to the ground, landing badly.

He got up.

He had to do it again, so he didn't hesitate. This time he paid more attention as he climbed over the maze wall. He could see The Claw Man standing there with the others, a megaphone in one hand and a gun in the other.

The Claw Man took aim as Ethan swung his legs over the top of the wall.

He fired.

Missed again.

Ethan dropped to the ground, once again landing badly. Was The Claw Man a terrible shot, or did he not want to ruin the fun by successfully shooting Ethan off the wall? Ethan suspected it was the latter.

There was the exit! Only about twenty feet away!

Kenny ran around the corner.

As Ethan got back to his feet, Kenny tackled him.

They both hit the ground.

Kenny scrambled to crawl right over Ethan as both men

desperately tried to move toward the exit. Kenny slammed Ethan's face into the ground, buying him a couple of seconds, but Ethan grabbed his foot.

They kept violently struggling, making forward progress only a couple of inches at a time. Ethan wasn't sure if the entire maze was being monitored or just the areas with the keys, but this had to be insanely entertaining to the people watching.

"What if we—?" Ethan started to ask, before Kenny slammed his face into the ground again.

As far as he knew, there was no time limit, so this could go on for a while.

He spat out some blood. "What about a tie?"

"What?" Kenny asked.

"A tie! If we both came out at the exact same time! What would they do?"

"Boil both of us."

They rolled into the wall.

Ethan punched him in the face.

Kenny let out a howl of pain that seemed excessive. He clutched at his eye and screamed.

There was no jelly on Ethan's knuckles or anything like that, but, yes, the punch to Kenny's face might very well have got him directly in the eye. Ethan's first deranged instinct was to ask him to pull his hand away so he could take a look. His second, much more rational instinct was to use this opportunity to get closer to the maze exit.

He rapidly crawled forward as Kenny bellowed.

Almost there.

Kenny grabbed his foot.

Ethan kicked him in the face. From the sound of it, he might have kicked Kenny in the eye again. Same eye? Different eye? No way to tell without looking back, and Ethan was focused entirely on the exit.

He reached the open gate.

Later he was sure he'd have nightmares about punching and kicking some poor guy in the eyes to win the challenge, but for now, he was happy that he'd get to see his wife and kids again.

Kenny got up and charged at him.

Ethan tried to gracefully step out of the maze, but toppled over and crashed to the ground instead.

He'd done it. He'd come in second.

Rick helped him up as Kenny stepped out of the maze as well. His right eye was closed, but nothing was leaking underneath the eyelid.

Lisa was seated on a lawn chair, a frozen drink in her hand.

The Claw Man lowered his megaphone. "It looks like Ethan Caustin may be our second place finisher. Hand me your keys."

Ethan took the four keys out of his pocket and gave them to him.

"Whoopsie," said The Claw Man. "Looks like we have a problem."

21

"What's the problem?" Ethan asked.

"You were supposed to find four blue keys," said The Claw Man. He held up one of them. "This one is turquoise."

"It's blue."

"Turquoise."

"Turquoise is blue," Ethan insisted. "It's light blue."

"It doesn't match the other keys."

"Nobody said it had to match the other keys. You said to find four blue keys. Those are four blue keys."

"You say blue. I say turquoise. Unfortunately for you, we have an imbalance of power here. My turquoise outranks your blue. Sorry."

Ethan couldn't believe what he was hearing. This was complete bullshit.

"Let's be fair," said Rick, stepping forward. "Turquoise is technically a shade of blue. He followed the instructions."

The Claw Man laughed. "Oh, hi, Rick. Hypocritical much? You were right there with us when we planned this out, and you loved the idea of tricking them with the colors of the keys. It may even have been your suggestion."

"It wasn't."

"Either way, you were totally on board until it came back to bite you in the ass."

"But turquoise is blue."

"No. Turquoise is turquoise. I'll put that on a bumper sticker for you." The Claw Man extended an open hand to Kenny. "Let's see what you've got."

Kenny, not looking happy, dropped three keys into The Claw Man's palm.

"Ooooh, same problem here," said The Claw Man, picking up one of them and holding it up for everybody to see. "This isn't green. This is olive."

A tall, thin woman with gray hair shook her head. "No, no, no." Ethan wondered if she served the same role for Kenny as Rick did for him. "Olive is green. That's why they call them green olives."

"Sorry, Christine, you were right there in the meeting with Rick and the rest of us. You thought it was a simply delightful idea. You can't start whining about it now."

"I didn't get to see the keys," said Christine. "Neither did Rick. If you'd shown me the olive-colored key and said that it wouldn't count as a green key, I would've argued the point I'm making now. It's clearly a green key. And it's clearly a blue key. When we discussed this in the design stage, we assumed that the keys would be different enough from the main color that you could definitively say 'This is not green' or 'This is not blue.'

That's not the case here. If you went up to people on the street and asked them what color these keys were, they'd say that they were blue and green, not turquoise and olive."

"What about Lisa?" asked The Claw Man. "You don't see her with a pink or a mauve key."

"That's because pink and mauve are considered individual colors," said Christine. Ethan liked her more than he liked Rick. "The keys that were placed in the maze don't follow the parameters of what we discussed in the meeting. This isn't our fault."

"Damn," said The Claw Man. "Kenny's got himself a top-notch attorney here. That said, your argument would not hold up in a court of law. When we discussed ways to make the maze more difficult, we came up with the idea of a wall of a thousand different keys that they had to search through. Somebody, I forget exactly who it was, proposed the idea that some of the keys would be close to the color that the players were supposed to find, as a way to trick them. Apparently it worked. Twice. The thing is, for a key to be *almost* the right color but not quite, there has to be some room for debate. If the key is far enough from green that everybody agrees that it's not a legitimately green key, then it wouldn't fool a player into taking it, and the whole idea would be pointless. Baked right there into the concept is the idea that there'd be a protest. So I reject your objections."

"Then what happens next?" asked Rick.

"They get their asses back into the maze to get the right key."

"No," said Christine. "Kenny was badly hurt. Look at how swollen his eye is. He wouldn't have put himself in the position to get injured that badly if he'd known the key was wrong. You announced through the megaphone that he'd found the key."

"I said that he found a key," said The Claw Man. "I didn't say he found the right key. My words were chosen very carefully."

"They were misleading."

"I think they should have to continue the race," said Rick.

"Well, of course *you* do," said The Claw Man, grinning. To Christine, he said, "We had a little incident with Rick here that forced us to change the stakes a bit. If Ethan goes into the oil, Rick goes in right after him. So, yeah, he *really* wants Ethan to win."

"Oh," said Christine.

"Let's send them back into the maze," said Rick. "It's the only fair way to do this."

"You can say that because your player isn't as badly injured," said Christine.

"What are you talking about? He's all slashed up."

"So is Kenny. And Kenny has an eye injury. He has no chance of winning if they go back into the maze."

"That's not my problem," said Rick.

"How about we call it a tie?" asked Christine. "Neither of them die, but neither of them get a point."

Rick nodded. "I'm fine with that."

"What about Lisa?" The Claw Man asked. "She ran through the maze thinking it was a matter of life or death. How is it fair to her if it turns out there was no real danger?"

"I'm totally okay with it being a tie between them," said Lisa.

The Claw Man looked around at everybody. "Is there anybody who objects to the idea of making it a tie between Ethan and Kenny?"

Nobody objected.

"Done!" he said. "It's officially a tie for second place."

Ethan almost collapsed with relief. He'd been too terrified to even breathe. Kenny looked more angry than relieved.

"Which means," The Claw Man continued, "that we have to do the tiebreaker."

"Wait, what?" Rick asked.

"Don't plead ignorance. We had a tiebreaker. We're going to flip a coin and see who comes in second place and who comes in third." He took a silver dollar out of his pocket.

Christine sighed. "I'm okay with the tiebreaker."

"I'm not!" said Rick. "This isn't what we agreed on!"

"Your objection has been noted," said The Claw Man. "Now I'd advise you to quit bellyaching and start trying to visualize winning the coin toss. Heads, Ethan wins. Tails, Kenny wins."

Ethan had no idea what to do. Should he continue to protest? Should he claim that he didn't trust the coin toss to be impartial, and that they needed to replace it with another method, like they had with the wheel in Rick's Vegas office? Should he just shut the hell up and hope that the 50/50 odds worked out in his favor?

He didn't think he could protest his way out of this.

The Claw Man flipped the coin into the air. He caught it, then slapped it down on his wrist.

"Before I reveal, I just want to say what an honor it's been to have both of you in this game," he said. "I mean that sincerely. We've had a couple of duds, and a couple of players we had to eliminate prematurely—you were there for one of those, right Ethan?—and so I appreciate what you've both given to the game. It will give me no pleasure to watch one of you die an agonizing death."

He lifted his hand just enough to peek underneath.

"The coin has made its decision," he said. "And before I announce it, I just want to give credit where it's due to the coin designers throughout history who've made it possible to break ties in this manner. Let's give it up for the coin designers, ladies and gentlemen!"

Everybody stood there, unsure whether he genuinely intended for them to applaud.

"I'm not kidding," said The Claw Man. "A round of applause for the coin designers of the world. Let's do this!"

Everybody around Ethan applauded, but he couldn't bring himself to join in the levity. He still hadn't figured out what he'd do if the coin toss didn't work out in his favor. He might as well fight as hard as he possibly could, since there wasn't much they could do to him that was worse than being boiled alive.

"I have bad news for one of you," The Claw Man said. He looked at Kenny. "Kenny, I hate to break this to you...but you have to play the next round."

He removed his hand, showing that the coin had landed on tails.

Two of the men, presumably anticipating that Ethan would try to make a run for it, grabbed him before he could move.

"If he struggles too much, pull his arm back until it snaps," said The Claw Man. "He'll stop."

Everybody followed as the men dragged Ethan over to the shed.

22

Rick had absolutely no idea what to do.

If he just let them dunk Ethan in the barrel of boiling oil, he'd be next. But what the hell could he do? Try to gently dissuade them from doing this? Turn into an action movie hero and perform a daring rescue, even though he was far outnumbered and everybody else was armed? What were the odds of success? A million to fucking one?

He followed the group to the shed.

Nobody was actually pointing a gun at him, but The Claw Man gave him a look that made it clear that he knew Rick might try something. And he might. A bullet to the skull would be better than the fate planned for him.

He watched helplessly as they snapped the handcuffs on Ethan.

"He's your player," said The Claw Man. "You do the honors."

Rick walked over and turned the crank. He tried to block out the sounds of Ethan's protests as the chain went taut and lifted him into the air. He turned another crank, which positioned Ethan directly above the barrel.

"Lisa, you can go inside," said The Claw Man. "We're still monitoring you, so don't try anything stupid. But as the first place finisher, you don't have to watch."

Lisa nodded and quickly left.

"Kenny, you're not so lucky. But you're luckier than Ethan. Ethan, you're leaving behind a wife and two sons, but we're not complete monsters." He took out a cell phone. "You get to record a goodbye video. Sixty seconds to say whatever you want to your family. I'll zoom in close so they don't see exactly what's going to happen to you."

The goodbye video. Rick had forgotten about that. It seemed really entertaining while they were discussing the various ways the game would play out. It was simultaneously kind-hearted, because it would give the family some closure, and mean-spirited, because it dragged out the victim's awareness of his nightmarish end. In the meeting room, eating doughnuts and sipping expensive coffee, it had seemed like it would be amusing.

Rick envisioned a scenario where he mightily kicked over the barrel of oil, surprising the onlookers so much that they didn't get out of the way in time. As the boiling oil rushed over their feet, they screamed out in pain and fell forward, sizzling their hands as well. The ones who remained standing would charge forward, but Ethan would swing forward and kick them, knocking them unconscious. Over in fifteen seconds.

Of course, it would take several people to push over that barrel, and they'd get severely burned doing it. This derring-do escape was entirely in Rick's imagination.

"FUCK YOU," Ethan told The Claw Man.

"That's not a very heartwarming message to your family."

"I'm not playing your game anymore."

"This is your chance to say goodbye."

"They know I love them. This video won't bring them any kind of peace. I'm not going to let you twist the knife any more. Fuck you."

The Claw Man didn't lower his phone. "You still get the full sixty seconds. Is that really how you want to use it?"

It really wasn't, but Ethan wasn't going to offer up some sappy video message for The Claw Man and the other sadists to laugh at. If they *did* send the video to Jenny—which he doubted—they'd probably add a wacky filter to it to make him look like a cartoon dog or something. If he had to die, it was going to be a defiant death.

Also, he knew that if he tried to deliver a sincere message to Jenny, Patrick, and Tim, he'd become a blubbering mess of sorrow and terror. Being an asshole right now was the only thing keeping him from completely breaking down.

"You sure that's how you want to go out?" The Claw Man asked. "I mean, you're an adult, it's your choice. I personally wouldn't want to bid farewell to my family that way, but you do you."

"Fuck you," Ethan told him.

The Claw Man lowered his phone. "All right, then. Rick, turn that crank."

Rick, looking physically ill, began to turn the crank. Ethan lifted his legs, trying to keep his feet out of the boiling oil.

No.

Screw this.

If Ethan could be defiant, then so could Rick. It was too late to save his player, but that didn't mean Rick had to be the one to kill him. He was done playing along.

Rick was under no impression that this somehow made him noble. His plan to make a break for it was cowardly, and he probably wouldn't even make it out of the shed, but at least he was taking charge of his own fate.

He stopped turning the crank and ran.

The Claw Man shot him in the knee.

Rick cried out in pain and fell to the ground. He didn't even have to look at the wound to know that he would not be getting back up.

"Why would you go and do that?" The Claw Man asked. "Now it's messy."

"He could do this to you," said Rick to the others, trying to speak instead of simply screaming. "There's no loyalty! I'm an employee just like the rest of you, and look what he's going to do to me! You could be next!"

"You broke the rules," said The Claw Man.

"He had no choice!" Ethan shouted. "What's going to happen to him could happen to any of you! That's the kind of people you work for!"

The Claw Man chuckled. "Everybody else knows not to break the rules."

"Like he said, I had no choice," said Rick. He could not *believe* how much it hurt to get shot in the knee. Maybe the boiling oil would've been better. "Things got out of control. I did what I had to do, and now I'm going to die for it."

The Claw Man chuckled again, though it was a bit forced, like he was trying to convey amusement and disdain that didn't quite exist. He pointed the gun at Rick's head.

ETHAN WATCHED as The Claw Man walked right up to Rick. He pressed the barrel of his gun right between Rick's eyes.

"You're babbling," said The Claw Man. "Nobody's interested in your nonsense. It's time for you to shut the fuck up."

He pulled the trigger.

Rick's dead body flopped over.

Everybody was silent.

The handcuffs were digging into Ethan's wrists and it was becoming more difficult to keep his knees bent and his feet out of the oil.

Rick lay on his side, blood seeping into the ground.

"What did he do?" Christine asked.

"You saw him," said The Claw Man. "He made a run for it."

"I mean, what did he do before that?"

"He fed inside information to his player. Tried to give him an unfair advantage. And, oh, yeah, he murdered Gavin and Butch when he thought they might tattle on him for violating the 'never bluff' rule. Instead of ending the game for Ethan here, we decided to make Rick's penalty the same as his. He got off pretty easy."

A trickle of blood ran down Ethan's arm. He wasn't sure if it came from his wrists, or one of the cuts that was already there. The pain was excruciating.

"He had a daughter," said Christine.

"I'm sorry, is there a problem, Christine?" The Claw Man asked.

"No, sir."

"Good. Let's not forget that we're still playing a game here. We all knew how this was going to work out in the end."

"For the players. Not the staff."

Ethan couldn't see The Claw Man's face, but from his body language Ethan assumed that his eyes narrowed. He took a step toward Christine. "Did you just give a spoiler?"

"No. That didn't spoil anything. What are you talking about?"

"My mistake. I don't like the grim mood that's happening here. We're supposed to be having fun. I guess Rick won't be turning any more cranks, but I need somebody to get in there and lower Ethan to his death. Kenny, do you want to do the honors?"

Kenny shook his head. "No."

"You sure?"

"I don't want to do it."

"All right. Nobody's going to make you. Any other volunteers? Should we send somebody inside to see if Lisa wants to do it?"

Ethan noticed that Christine was reaching behind her back. Was she going for a gun?

Holy shit! Yes! She took out a gun and pointed it at The Claw Man.

A gunshot rang out and part of Christine's scalp came off.

As Christine dropped, everybody except The Claw Man started looking around to see where the shot had come from.

The man whose name Ethan didn't know, but who he assumed was Lisa's equivalent of Rick or Christine, hurried into the shed as he took out a gun of his own. He spun around and fired at The Claw Man. A spray of blood shot from The Claw Man's side and he fell to his knees.

Ethan didn't know how much longer he could keep his legs out of the boiling oil.

Kenny put his hands in the air. "Don't shoot!" he shouted. "Don't shoot!"

The Claw Man took out his own gun as the man who'd shot at him moved out of Ethan's line of sight. Ethan thought he was trying to hide behind the barrel.

Both of them fired off a few shots.

At least one of The Claw Man's shots struck the barrel. Oil started to pour out, but it was a thin trickle. Ethan's legs would give out long before enough drained from the barrel to make a difference.

Ethan could hear movement behind him, and no grunts of pain, so as far as he knew the other man was still alive and well.

Kenny remained paralyzed, face contorted with fear as if he expected to get shot in the head at any moment.

The man behind Ethan squeezed off another shot. Got The Claw Man in the other side. The Claw Man placed each of his hands over a wound, not dropping the gun as he did so. He looked dizzy and disoriented.

Ethan couldn't hold up his legs anymore. They swung down and the soles of his shoes dipped into the oil. He immediately bent them at the knees again. He was in absolute agony, and it felt like his hands might simply tear off at the wrists and send him plunging into the oil, but there was a chance that if this gunfight worked out in his favor, somebody would set him free.

The man came out of his hiding spot. Instead of shooting The Claw Man again, he ran over and kicked him in the chest, knocking him onto his back. He grabbed The Claw Man's gun then hurried to edge of the shed and opened fire.

Somebody screamed. It sounded like they might be on the roof.

Their scream got closer.

Ethan heard a thump, which he was pretty sure was a sniper falling off the roof.

Kenny lowered his hands. He began to walk toward Ethan.

"What are you doing?" asked the man.

"Getting him down."

"Nah. Let him die. He's no good to me. And neither are you."

The man shot Kenny in the face.

Four dead bodies, plus The Claw Man. Jesus Christ.

The man walked out of the shed. Then he immediately stopped. "Aw, shit," he muttered.

Yet another gunshot. Blood spurted from the man's chest and he fell to the ground.

He lay there, writhing, gasping for breath. Lisa, holding the gun she'd won for completing the maze in first place, walked over to him. She pointed the gun at him, then shook her head. "I'd be stupid if I wasted a bullet," she informed him.

"Please get me down!" said Ethan.

Lisa hurried over to him. She turned the crank until Ethan was no longer positioned over the barrel, then turned the other crank to lower him. As his feet touched the ground, it was clear that his legs weren't going to be able to come close to supporting his weight, so he just let her lower him until he was sitting.

She removed his handcuffs. Ethan's arms flopped to his sides. Yes, the blood had come from them digging into his wrists, so right now he was thankful that there was no feeling in them.

"Good thing the cuffs weren't locked," she said. "I'd have had to shoot your hands off."

Ethan wasn't sure if she was joking or not. He didn't care.

"Is everybody dead?" he asked.

"The drivers are still inside. Everybody else is dead or dying, as far as I know. Look, I need to get going. My fiancé could be in serious danger, and I can't drag you around, so good luck to you."

She hurried off.

Ethan inspected his wrists more closely. They were in bad shape but he didn't need to rush off to the emergency room. If he wrapped them up he'd be fine for a while.

For now, all he could do is sit here helplessly until the feeling came back into his limbs.

The pins and needles feeling started soon. He wondered why it was called "pins and needles," when either pins or needles alone would describe the sensation. Then he wondered why he was thinking about something so trivial. Was he losing more blood than he thought? He needed to stay laser-focused on the problem at hand.

Now the pins and needles were absolute agony, closer to the sensation of a homicidal maniac stabbing his arms and legs with a knife over and over and over. The pain was unreal. At least it would be over soon, as long as his ordeal hadn't caused permanent damage.

The torture began to relent.

Finally he was able to crawl. He couldn't tell if the man Lisa had shot was still alive—he wasn't moving—but The Claw Man was still alive and conscious, though he wouldn't be putting up much of a fight.

Ethan went over to Rick's body, reached into his pocket, and took out his cell phone. He tapped at the screen. The phone was locked with face ID, but hopefully his face wasn't mangled enough to stop it from working. Ethan held the phone up to his dead face, and the phone unlocked.

He called Jenny.

She answered immediately. "Hello?"

"It's me."

"Oh, thank God."

"I know we've already been through this, but get out of the house. Get the kids in the car and just drive. Don't call the police unless I tell you to. Just go."

"Are you okay?"

"I'm fine."

"What's happening?"

Ethan thought about his answer for a moment. "I think I'm about to hijack a plane."

23

Ethan kind of wished he hadn't shared that information with Jenny. It would generate a lot of very reasonable questions that he didn't have time to answer right now.

"I'll get the kids out of the house," said Jenny, apparently deciding that ignorance was bliss for now.

"I'll call you as soon as I can. I love you."

"I love you."

Ethan hung up. He either needed to cut off Rick's head and bring it along, or disable the face ID on the phone, so he went with the latter.

He managed to stand up. He picked up The Claw Man's and Christine's guns. He assumed the van drivers had heard all of the shots, but he didn't know if they were the kind of guys to flee, call for help, or prepare an ambush. He wished he could worry about them now, but he had a more pressing concern.

He crouched down next to The Claw Man, then pushed the

barrel of one of the guns against his chin. "Take out your phone," Ethan told him.

"You're a dead man."

"I said, take out your phone."

"The boiling oil is nothing compared to what's going to happen to you."

"I need you alive," said Ethan. "So if you don't want me to shoot you in the ankle, take out your phone."

The Claw Man shoved his bloody hand into his pocket and pulled out a cell phone.

"Call your partners. Tell them to end the game."

"They won't."

"Then that will be really bad for you. I'd try to make a good case for it. Tell them to put everything on hold—and I mean *everything*, especially going after family members—and that you'll be there to discuss it in person."

The Claw Man tapped at his screen. "It's not working," he said.

"Wipe the blood off your fingers."

The Claw Man wiped his fingers off on his pants, then tapped at the screen again.

"Put it on speaker," Ethan told him.

"What the hell is going on?" asked a man on the other end.

"We've got a little bit of a situation here. I'm going to need you to put the game on pause. Everything, including penalties."

"How did you let this happen?"

"Are you going to interrogate me or are you going to pause the fucking game?"

"We'll pause the game. But we told you to—"

"Save the lecture, okay? We'll talk about this when I get there. Goodbye." The Claw Man hung up. "Now what?"

"Now I'm going to see if the drivers are still here. Try not to bleed out before I get back."

Ethan cautiously walked out of the shed. He didn't see anybody on the roof, so he hurried over to the house then went inside. The van driver was still seated on the living room couch, watching a courtroom show. Another man who looked about ninety sat next to him.

"Uh, hi," said Ethan.

The driver looked over at him. "Hi."

"You didn't hear all the gunfire?"

"Our job is to wait for instructions, not go out and get ourselves shot."

"Well, good. The Claw Man has been seriously injured. I'm going to need you to help get him in the van, then take us to his private jet."

"Are you asking nicely, or should I assume that you're going to point that gun at me if I say no?"

"For now, let's say that I'm asking nicely."

The driver nodded and stood up. He handed the remote control to the other driver.

They walked out of the house. The driver seemed unimpressed by the sight of all of the dead bodies. He looked down at The Claw Man. "Those are some nasty wounds," he said. "We probably shouldn't move him."

"We're going to move him," said Ethan.

"Just help him," said The Claw Man. "It's fine."

"It's gonna hurt."

"I know it's gonna fucking hurt! It already hurts!"

"Do you want heads or tails?" the driver asked Ethan.

"Tails."

Ethan picked up The Claw Man by the feet, which was unbelievably painful on his injured wrists, and the driver lifted him under his shoulders. The Claw Man cried out in pain, though the amount of sympathy this elicited from Ethan was minimal. They carried him around the house and over to the van.

"I'll put the seats down so he can lie on the floor," said the driver. "Should we get a blanket or some garbage bags or something so he doesn't bleed all over the upholstery?"

"Fuck the upholstery!" said The Claw Man. "Let's just go!"

They were as careful as possible when getting him into the back of the van. Ethan didn't care about his comfort, but if The Claw Man got jostled and some intestines or a kidney became visible, he'd be less useful as a hostage.

As the driver sped them to a small airport, The Claw Man called to let them know he was on his way. They were flying back to Las Vegas.

They were somehow able to drive right up to the plane. The ability to bypass all lines was a major incentive for Ethan to become incredibly rich.

THE CLAW MAN was getting blood all over his seat.

There was no beverage service on this flight, because Ethan had ordered the crew to stay in the cockpit and not come out for any reason. He wasn't sure if he'd actually shoot them or not. If he missed, he could depressurize the cabin and kill everybody—

or so he assumed, since he didn't know exactly how the science on that worked. He was relatively certain that shooting a gun midflight was bad.

"You ruined everything," The Claw Man told him.

"My bad."

"We were almost at the final challenge. All of the players in one building. Fight to the death. Winner takes all. A five million dollar prize to the winner. It would've been spectacular."

"I'm sure everybody involved is very disappointed."

"We had six floors of content. Traps everywhere. Getting enough scorpions for the maze was a pain in the ass, but that's nothing compared to the surprises in the final building. We had a fucking lion. Do you know how much work and expense we put into that building? If I showed you some of the design documents, you'd want to jump right back into the game."

"You should calm down," said Ethan. "You're getting overly agitated and when you twist around like that it makes you bleed more."

"I was even rooting for you," said The Claw Man. "I thought to myself, that guy can pull this off. You could've been five million dollars richer. Now it's no prizes for anyone. All the risks everybody took, all the lies they had to tell to their significant others, all the players who died during the game...all for nothing. Thanks a fucking lot, Ethan."

"I'm truly not sure why you think I'm going to feel guilty about this."

"Because you ruined the game!"

"You are one out of touch guy."

"It's not just about you. You should think about others."

"So what were the points all about?" Ethan asked.

"Before the final battle started, the players could use their points in exchange for weapons and advantages. Let's say you've got three points. Do you use them all for a machine gun, or do you spend a point on a six-shooter, a point on a bulletproof vest, and a point on a peek at a map that shows you the location of the hidden passages? Each player would have to make their own decisions."

"Sorry I'm missing out."

"There's no rule saying players can't combine their points. And yet it's a zero sum game with only one winner. Is it best to form alliances and use teamwork to make it closer to the end? Three players working together could wipe out the rest of the competition, and then worry about turning on each other when the time came. But maybe it's better to play it solo, so you're a smaller target. Stay under the radar. Lots of factors to consider if you're going to win this thing. It tests your mental abilities as well as physical. People working behind the scenes put their *soul* into this experience that you're trying to shut down."

"Well, I've never been on a private jet before, and you're ruining the experience."

"Rick should never have chosen you."

"I agree."

A LIMOUSINE WAS WAITING for them when they landed at a small airport near Las Vegas. There were sheets on the seats. Ethan had never been in a limo, either, but he wasn't inclined to make use of the minibar or the ability to open up the roof and put his head outside.

After a short drive, the limo pulled into a parking garage.

"Call and let them know we're here," said Ethan.

"They know we're here."

"Tell them I'll shoot you if they try anything."

"They know that too."

"Make sure they know how serious I am."

"You get that they're listening right now, right?"

"And I also want you to know how serious I am. I will kill you without hesitation."

"Noted," said The Claw Man. "Now can we please get the fuck out of the limo so I can get some proper medical attention?"

The parking garage had a private entrance to the meeting spot, sparing Ethan and the limo driver the need to carry a blood-covered man down the street. The door buzzed as they approached—apparently they were indeed being watched—and they awkwardly opened it and brought The Claw Man inside.

Mindy, the receptionist from the office where Ethan had gotten into this shitstorm, stood up from behind her desk as they entered. "Let me get the other door for you," she said. "They're right in there."

"Thank you," said Ethan.

As she went over to the door, he told the driver to set The Claw Man down. Ethan then pulled The Claw Man to his feet, stood behind him, and held the gun against the side of his head in the traditional hostage manner.

Mindy opened the door. Ethan and The Claw Man went inside.

The room was lined with monitors. Dozens upon dozens of them. Lots of views of various homes from the outside, and shots of rooms from the inside. He recognized his own bedroom.

They'd had an excellent view of him pretending to have sex with Jenny.

The center of the room was occupied by a long desk, the kind you'd find in an executive boardroom. There were about twenty chairs, all of them unoccupied except the two at the far end. Two middle-aged men sat there. They looked unhappy.

Mindy shut the door behind them.

Ethan didn't want The Claw Man to lose consciousness and fall, so he plopped him down in the closest chair, keeping the gun to his head.

"Don't make me kill him," Ethan said.

"We won't," said one of the men. "We understand that you're very perturbed right now, and we hope we can work this out."

"I hope so, too."

"I am The Duke of Amusement. My partner here is Enigmaticus. And you've obviously met The Claw Man. So what can we do for you, Ethan?"

"I want you to stop the game. I want you to leave me and my family alone."

The Duke nodded. "And if we don't indulge your request, you will shoot The Claw Man in the head, right?"

"Right."

"Well, this is a bit of a conundrum. On the one hand, we certainly don't want you to kill him. He's not just a business partner, he's a friend. On the other hand, we put a lot of work into this game, and we don't want some player barging in here and telling us we have to end it all."

"This isn't a bluff," said Ethan.

"Oh, I'm sure it's not. You wouldn't force your way onto a private jet and fly out here just to bluff. You could be speeding away with your family right now. They're making good time. Tim got to sit in the front seat, even though he's younger."

Ethan almost wanted to squeeze the trigger right now. Kill The Claw Man then try to take out the other two before they were able to retaliate. He resisted the urge.

"Here's the deal," said Enigmaticus. "We don't have the ability to stop you from killing The Claw Man if you really want to. From there, you'll try to shoot at us, but we wouldn't have let you into our office if we didn't think we could take you out before that happened. So you're dead, our partner is dead, and it's just an unpleasant situation for everybody. No real winners in this scenario, and what fun is a game without a winner, right?"

"I guess," said Ethan. If he took a shot at one of them before killing The Claw Man, he might have the element of surprise on his side, but he had to admit that there wasn't really a plausible outcome where he was the only one alive. He needed them to decide that saving The Claw Man's life was worth ending the game.

"The game is basically ruined at this point," said Enigmaticus. "We had this whole thing planned where—"

"He told me about it on the plane," said Ethan.

"I know, I know. We just put a lot of work into it. There was this one trap where...well, it doesn't matter. Maybe in Game Two," he said, wistfully.

"I really, truly, wholeheartedly do not care that you're missing out on watching all of us kill each other," said Ethan.

"Fair enough, fair enough."

"So let us be perfectly clear," said The Duke. "We are not willing to shut down the game just because you're threatening to kill our friend. I'm sure he agrees with our decision. But we'd also like to avoid a bloodbath. Therefore, we're going to let you participate in a final round. All or nothing. The odds are 50/50. Everything on one spin of the wheel."

"What do I win?"

"You win an end to the game. All challenges will immediately cease. The remaining players will still be under a gag order with no expiration date, but they'll each receive one hundred thousand dollars for their trouble. The families of the deceased players will receive one hundred thousand dollars as well. You, as the player taking the risk, will receive one million dollars, along with the guaranteed safety of Jenny, Patrick, and Tim."

"And if I lose?"

"We'll kill you, your family, and all of the remaining players."

"It won't be as bad as being lowered into boiling oil," said Enigmaticus. "We'll just shoot you. Quick and easy. Your family won't suffer, either. Headshots, if possible. Nothing where they linger."

"That doesn't work for me."

"What's your counter-offer?"

"You kill me. My family and the other players go free."

"Can't do it," said Enigmaticus. "Not for 50/50 odds. If you want a game where your family survives, no matter what, the odds have to change."

"How about one in three?" asked The Duke. "Same prize if you win. If you lose, you're the only one to die."

"This offer expires in one minute," said The Duke.

"I accept," said Ethan.

He wished he had some brilliant plan. Some way to twist everything in his favor. But he didn't. All Ethan had was his willingness to give himself a two-in-three chance of getting shot in order to guarantee the safety of his wife and children.

"Oh, good," said The Duke. "This'll be fun."

"I'm not spinning the wheel," said Ethan. "It could be rigged. I'll write a number on a piece of paper. You guess if it's one, two, or three."

Enigmaticus shook his head. "Uh-uh. I'll write the number. Then I'll slide the paper away from me so you can see that it's undisturbed. You guess the number. If you're right, you win. If you're wrong, you lose. Fair?"

"Fair."

"I've got a pen and paper right here," said Enigmaticus. He slid them off the table and onto his lap, and then began to write.

Ethan tensed up, waiting for him to have a gun in his hand when he showed it again.

He didn't. He had a folded piece of paper. He slid it toward Ethan. The desk was far too long for Ethan to reach it, but he could at least see that there was no funny business going on with the slip of paper.

"I didn't write numbers," said Enigmaticus. "I either drew a pumpkin, a house, or a bunny. Which is it?"

Ethan stared at the paper, as if he might suddenly develop X-ray vision and be able to read it.

This was a terrible idea. He should just shoot The Claw Man and try to shoot the others.

No. If he did that, they'd go after Jenny and the kids. He had to play the game. One in three odds weren't bad.

Was Enigmaticus more likely to draw a pumpkin, a house, or a bunny?

He'd expect him to guess bunny for sure. Or maybe

pumpkin. Those were funny sounding words. He wouldn't expect him to guess house.

Or would he expect Ethan to follow this exact line of reasoning and go with the most generic choice?

Pumpkin, house, or bunny?

"You drew a house," Ethan said.

"I'm going to need you to put down the gun before the reveal," said Enigmaticus. "We can't have you going on a shooting spree if you lose."

"You'll be unharmed if you win," The Duke assured him. "We don't cheat."

Ethan had no choice but to trust them. He dropped the gun onto the floor.

"Do you want to open the paper or do you want me to?" asked Enigmaticus.

"I'll do it."

Ethan walked over and picked up the paper. Please let it be a house. He took a deep breath.

He unfolded the paper.

24

"Fuckin' bunny," Ethan muttered.

He dropped the paper onto the desk.

"Best two out of three?" he asked.

EPILOGUE

"Everything is going to be okay," Jenny promised Patrick and Tim, even though she knew no such thing. She had no destination. No plan. Just drive until she heard from Ethan again.

If she ever did. Nobody was answering the phone he'd called from.

She'd give him until nightfall before she started to make plans to get out of the country without him.

HER PHONE RANG. The call was from Rick Oddsmaker, as it had been the last time Ethan called. She almost swerved off the road in her haste to answer.

"Hello?"

"It's me."

"Oh, thank God. Where are you?"

"I'm in Las Vegas," said Ethan.

"Did you...did you hijack a plane?"

"Kind of. Depends on your definition of hijack. I'm calling to say that everything is okay. We're out of danger now. You can go back home."

"How do you know?"

"Because I won the game. I mean, I won the revised version of the game, and I only won because they were nice enough to play two out of three. I guessed that he drew a duckie, and then I guessed that he drew a banjo."

"I don't understand what you're talking about," Jenny said.

"I know. I've lost a lot of blood and I'm feeling kind of scatterbrained right now and I'm probably not making sense. I'm going to be completely honest with you about everything from now on, so I'll tell you that for them to give me a second chance, I had to give up the opportunity for a million-dollar prize. But we've still got the fifty thousand, so that's good."

"You promise we're safe?"

"I promise. They don't cheat. I won fair and square. We did have to renegotiate the terms, though. I worked it out so you and the kids were always going to be safe no matter how it turned out, so that was nice, and I forfeited the chance at a million dollars, so that was less nice, but I get a salary now."

"A salary?"

"Yeah."

"Why do you get a salary, Ethan?"

"They like my work ethic. This was basically just the practice round, and since Rick is dead now, part of the conditions of my game were that I'd take his job if I won. Way better than getting shot in the head, right? I start training in a couple of weeks.

Would be sooner, but they're giving me time for the wounds to heal."

"I'm really confused."

"That's okay. Come on home. We'll talk about it tonight. Maybe we'll pop open that champagne."

— The End —

ACKNOWLEDGMENTS

Thanks to my usual amazing team of Tod Clark, Donna Fitzpatrick, Paul Goblirsch, Lynne Hansen, Michael McBride, Jim Morey, Mike Myers, Rhonda Rettig, and Paul Synuria II for their help with this novel.

BOOKS BY JEFF STRAND

Allison. She can break your bones using her mind. And she's trying very hard not to hurt you.

Wolf Hunt 3. George, Lou, Ally, and Eugene are back in another werewolf-laden adventure.

Clowns Vs. Spiders. Choose your side!

My Pretties. A serial kidnapper may have met his match in the two young ladies who walk the city streets at night, using themselves as bait...

Five Novellas. A compilation of *Stalking You Now, An Apocalypse of Our Own, Faint of Heart, Kutter,* and *Facial.*

Ferocious. The creatures of the forest are dead...and hungry!

Bring Her Back. A tale of revenge and madness.

Sick House. A home invasion from beyond the grave.

Bang Up. A filthy comedic thriller. "You want to pay me to sleep with your wife?" is just the start of the story.

Cold Dead Hands. Ten people are trapped in a freezer during a terrorist attack on a grocery store.

How You Ruined My Life (Young Adult). Sixteen-year-old Rod has a pretty cool life until his cousin Blake moves in and slowly destroys everything he holds dear.

Everything Has Teeth. A third collection of short tales of horror and macabre comedy.

An Apocalypse of Our Own. Can the Friend Zone survive the end of the world?

Stranger Things Have Happened (Young Adult). Teenager Marcus Millian III is determined to be one of the greatest magicians who ever lived. Can he make a live shark disappear from a tank?

Cyclops Road. When newly widowed Evan Portin gives a woman named Harriett a ride out of town, she says she's on a cross-country journey to slay a Cyclops. Is she crazy, or...?

Blister. While on vacation, cartoonist Jason Tray meets the town legend, a hideously disfigured woman who lives in a shed.

The Greatest Zombie Movie Ever (Young Adult). Three best friends with more passion than talent try to make the ultimate zombie epic.

Kumquat. A road trip comedy about TV, hot dogs, death, and obscure fruit.

I Have a Bad Feeling About This (Young Adult). Geeky, non-athletic Henry Lambert is sent to survival camp, which is bad enough *before* the trio of murderous thugs show up.

Pressure. What if your best friend was a killer...and he wanted you to be just like him? Bram Stoker Award nominee for Best Novel.

Dweller. The lifetime story of a boy and his monster. Bram Stoker Award nominee for Best Novel.

A Bad Day For Voodoo. A young adult horror/comedy about why sticking pins in a voodoo doll of your history teacher isn't always the best idea. Bram Stoker Award nominee for Best Young Adult Novel.

Dead Clown Barbecue. A collection of demented stories about severed noses, ventriloquist dummies, giant-sized vampires, sibling stabbings, and lots of other messed-up stuff.

Dead Clown Barbecue Expansion Pack. A few more stories for those who couldn't get enough.

Wolf Hunt. Two thugs for hire. One beautiful woman. And one vicious frickin' werewolf.

Wolf Hunt 2. New wolf. Same George and Lou.

The Sinister Mr. Corpse. The feel-good zombie novel of the year.

Benjamin's Parasite. A rather disgusting action/horror/comedy about why getting infected with a ghastly parasite is unpleasant.

Fangboy. A dark and demented fairy tale for adults.

Facial. Greg has just killed the man he hired to kill one of his wife's many lovers. Greg's brother desperately needs a dead body. It's kind of related to the lion corpse that he found in his basement. This is the normal part of the story.

Kutter. A serial killer finds a Boston terrier, and it might just make him into a better person.

Faint of Heart. To get her kidnapped husband back, Melody has to relive her husband's nightmarish weekend, step-by-step...and survive.

Mandibles. Giant killer ants wreaking havoc in the big city!

Stalking You Now. A twisty-turny thriller soon to be the feature film *Mindy Has To Die.*

Graverobbers Wanted (No Experience Necessary). First in the Andrew Mayhem series.

Single White Psychopath Seeks Same. Second in the Andrew Mayhem series.

Casket For Sale (Only Used Once). Third in the Andrew Mayhem series.

Lost Homicidal Maniac (Answers to "Shirley"). Fourth in the Andrew Mayhem series.

Suckers (with JA Konrath). Andrew Mayhem meets Harry McGlade. Which one will prove to be more incompetent?

Gleefully Macabre Tales. A collection of thirty-two demented tales. Bram Stoker Award nominee for Best Collection.

Elrod McBugle on the Loose. A comedy for kids (and adults who were warped as kids).

The Haunted Forest Tour (with Jim Moore). The greatest theme park attraction in the world! Take a completely safe ride through an actual haunted forest! Just hope that your tram doesn't break down, because this forest is PACKED with monsters...

Draculas (with JA Konrath, Blake Crouch, and F. Paul Wilson). An outbreak of feral vampires in a secluded hospital. This one isn't much like *Twilight.*

For information on all of these books, visit Jeff Strand's more-or-less official website at http://www.jeffstrand.com

Subscribe to Jeff Strand's free monthly newsletter (which includes a brand-new original short story in every issue) at http://eepurl.com/bpv5br

And remember:

Readers who leave reviews deserve great big hugs!

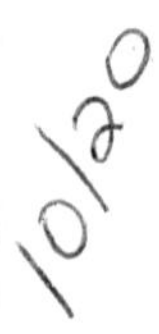

CPSIA information can be obtained
at www.ICGtesting.com
Printed in the USA
LVHW051637201020
669305LV00003B/781